She touched his hand. "Fantastic show."

"I'm glad you enjoyed it." He inhaled the soft scent of her perfume.

"I thought that last song was especially moving." She looked into his eyes, waiting.

Looks like she's on to me. "I wrote it. It was inspired by you." He reached out, tracing a gentle finger along her silken jaw.

She trembled beneath his touch. "I don't know what to say—it's beautiful."

He hopped down from the stage, never tearing his eyes from hers.

She came to him, and he enfolded her in his embrace. He lifted her chin, watched her eyes slide closed. Her glossy lips parted in sweet invitation. Leaning down, he pressed his lips to hers.

Her delicate fingers stroked the back of his neck as the kiss deepened.

He groaned, pulling her in as close as he could. He left her lips to explore the hollow of her neck, scented with the sweet, sensual notes of her perfume. His arousal grew, increasing to the point of pain. If he didn't have her tonight, he seriously thought he might explode.

He placed a parting kiss on her neck, then whispered in her ear. "Let's get out of here, or I'm going to make love to you on the stage—"

Dear Reader,

Thank you so much for picking up a copy of *This Tender Melody*. I'm so excited about my Harlequin Kimani Romance debut and I hope you are, as well. This story has been with me for quite a few years. I'd always wanted to write something that combined my two favorite things: romance and great music. The Gentlemen of Queen City series will bring you hot, sexy love stories, interwoven with the jazz music that shaped today's hits, all set in the sultry city of Charlotte, NC.

The heroes of these books are members of a jazz quartet. Four men who have little else in common are drawn together by their love of the music. Darius Winstead, the band's bassist, is up first, and he's about to meet his perfect match in technology executive Eve Franklin. Get ready—it's going to be a wild ride!

All the best,

Kianna

Facebook.com/KiannaWrites
Twitter.com/KiannaWrites

This Tender Melody

KIANNA ALEXANDER

HARLEQUIN® KIMANI™ ROMANCE

Recycling programs for this product may not exist in your area.

ISBN-13: 978-0-373-86424-9

This Tender Melody

For questions and comments about the quality of this book please contact us at CustomerService@Harlequin.com.

Printed in U.S.A.

Kianna Alexander, like any good Southern belle, wears many hats: loving wife, doting mama, advice-dispensing sister and gabbing girlfriend. She's a voracious reader, an amateur seamstress and occasional painter in oils. Chocolate, American history, sweet tea and Idris Elba are a few of her favorite things. A native of the Tar Heel state, Kianna still lives there with her husband, two kids and a collection of well-loved vintage '80s Barbie dolls.

Books by Kianna Alexander

Harlequin Kimani Romance

This Tender Melody

Dedication

For my son, whose bravery, curiosity and positive outlook inspire me daily.

Acknowledgments

First, I acknowledge my Creator, who lovingly made me, and gave me the gift of words.

Next, I declare my love to my family. To my husband, Keith, whose affection and support cradle my very soul, thank you. And to the two beautiful children born from our union, Mama loves you dearly.

I'd like to thank my "Council of Queens." These are the women who have lived a bit longer than me, whose love, support and advice help me make my way in the world. They are Lillie Mae and Gwen Mckinnon, Jettlean Pettiford, Joyce Manning, Henrietta Wyatt, Virginia Stone and the venerable Beverly Jenkins. I'd also like to express my love and gratitude to my wonderful street team, The Reading Roses, and to my Hot MAMA compatriots: Altonya Washington, Angie Daniels, Bridget Midway, Cheris Hodges, Denise Jeffries, Di Topaz, Iris Bolling, Loretta Walls, Reese Ryan and Yvette Hines. And all my love to the book clubs and readers who've been supporting my work since I first published in 2009.

Chapter 1

Holding a glass of iced tea, Eve Franklin strolled into the family room of her childhood home. Sundays with her parents were a sacred tradition, one that she never neglected in favor of her career or social life. Some of her girlfriends complained about her refusal to go on weekend escapades with them, lamenting that she saw enough of her parents when she went to work every day. Though she did work in the family business as chief financial officer of Franklin Technologies, Incorporated, she rarely saw her parents for more than a few minutes during a typical workday.

Her best friend, Lina, and some of her book club gal pals had taken off for the beach that weekend. Living in Charlotte, North Carolina, meant the best of both worlds—half a day's drive to the east or west delivered one to the majestic peaks of the mountains or the shimmering beauty of the Crystal Coast. Despite Lina's whining, protesting and threats, she'd reminded the girls that Sundays were irrevocably reserved for her parents. As she settled into her early thirties, her parents' advancing age wasn't lost on her. She wanted to spend as much time with them as she could manage.

By now, the group was no doubt "cutting up" at Lina's rental property on Emerald Isle. But she quickly pushed the thought aside. She was right where she was meant to be—where she most wanted to be and she knew she'd made the right decision.

Fading sunlight streamed in through the opened gold brocade drapes, illuminating the coffee table where a game of Monopoly was set up. The surround sound music system filled the large room with the sounds of instrumental jazz. The current piece featured the peppy strains of an acoustic guitar, the light airy notes of a flute and the accompaniment of a piano, while a plucked bass drove the beat.

The plush fibers of the midnight-navy carpet cushioned her bare feet as she crossed the room. She set the glass down on the short-legged mahogany coffee table, careful of the game board that already occupied the space. She used her hands to tug the hem of her yellow knee-length sundress. Reclaiming her seat on the floor, she grabbed her glass and took a sip. "Whose move is it?"

"My turn." Her mother, Louise, grabbed the pair of dice from the center of the game board. Shaking them inside her closed fist, she tossed the dice out, and then moved her iron-shaped game piece. "Your turn, Joseph."

Eve's gaze landed on her father's face, and she couldn't help but notice how drawn he looked. His face was a mask of exhaustion, and a bit of moisture clung to the edge of his graying hairline. The brown eyes she'd looked into all her life were now lacking the sparkle she was accustomed to seeing there. Now he looked ahead, almost as if looking through her, his expression vacant. "Daddy? It's your move."

He blinked, then offered her a smile. "Sorry, baby. Guess I checked out for a minute." He picked up the dice, drawing them close to his lips, and blew on them for luck.

Eve shifted her gaze to her mother, who also viewed him with concern. Joseph Franklin was a hard worker, always had been. He'd taken the reigns at a struggling software company in the early seventies, reshaped and restructured it, and made it into a powerhouse business. The years of labor he'd put in to turn FTI into a successful multinational software firm were beginning to take a toll on his health.

"Daddy, you look like you could use a nap." She kept her tone light and casual, wanting to avoid setting off his notorious stubborn streak.

"I'm fine." He set his car-shaped game piece on the designated spot and drew a card from one of the two piles on the board. "Looks like I won a beauty contest. Seventy-five dollars, please, Mrs. Banker." He showed his card to Louise, who smiled as she counted out the multicolored fake bills from the plastic tray.

She could see right through her father's attempt to change the subject. "Really, Daddy. You look tired. I don't want you overdoing it."

He groaned. "Baby, I appreciate your concern but I'm fine. I'm not about to quit now—not before you land on one of my properties with a hotel." He gestured to a few spots on the game board. "Then you're gonna owe me some serious cash."

She knew better than to press her father, so she looked to her mother for support.

Louise handed over the rainbow-colored stack of money she'd counted out for him. "Maybe she's right, honey. Sunday is the day of rest, after all, and we've got a busy day tomorrow. A little extra sleep couldn't hurt."

His face twisted into a frown and he lay his winnings down on the coffee table. "All right. If it'll get you two off my case, then I'll take a nap." He scooted to the edge of the sofa, then used his hands to brace himself as he got into a standing position. "You girls are always sending me to bed lately. Next, you'll be trying to goad me into retiring."

Louise blinked, her eyes darting away from her husband's accusing gaze.

Eve drew a deep breath. Her father was almost seventy years old, well past the age most people would have retired, especially considering the financial security he enjoyed. She knew better than to point out his age, but she didn't think retiring was a terrible idea. It was doubtful he'd even consider it, so she chose a different approach. "We're just trying to take good care of you, Daddy. You think about work too much."

He folded his arms across his chest, rumpling the striped fabric of his button-down shirt. "And you'd better be glad I do, otherwise we wouldn't be enjoying this lifestyle." He gestured around the room as if to draw her attention toward the expensive oil paintings, brass fixtures and other material possessions around the space.

While all the things they owned were very nice, and she did enjoy having a measure of financial security and freedom, none of that mattered to her nearly as much as her father's well-being. "You know we appreciate all your hard work. I just don't want you to worry. When the time comes, I'll be ready to take over at FTI."

Silence fell in the room. She knew she'd taken a risk by bringing up her eventual assumption of the CEO position, but she hadn't expected this. Studying her father's face, she found it unreadable. Was he confused or feeling out of sorts due to whatever was ailing him? Or did he doubt her ability to lead the company? She couldn't tell, but she didn't dare ask.

"I don't want to talk about this now. I'm going to bed." He turned around and stalked down the hallway, his hands formed into fists at his sides.

Once he was gone, she helped her mother tidy up. When the board game had been put away, she followed her mother into the kitchen and asked the question that was burning in her mind.

"Mama, what's wrong with Daddy?"

She shrugged. "I wish I knew. I've been trying to get him to go to the doctor for two solid weeks now." She rolled up the sleeves of her blue shirtdress, and turned on the tap to wash out the glasses they'd used.

Her mother's words made her nervous. If her mother couldn't get him to go see a doctor, she knew her own chances were pretty slim. Still, there was no way around the worry she felt regarding him. Maybe she was being overly cautious, but where her father's health was concerned, she'd much rather be persistent with her requests for him to see a doctor than find out too late that something was wrong.

With the three glasses set upside down to dry, Eve followed Louise back into the family room. Every inch of the house was filled with sweet memories of her childhood. As an only child of a well-off family, it was pretty likely she'd been overindulged. What mattered most to her, though, was the love her parents had showered her with at every given opportunity. They'd always made time for her, and that was the best gift she could have received, more precious to her than a boatload of jewels. "We have to make him go in for a physical. Something is wrong, I just know it."

Louise sat down on the sofa and sighed. "I know it, too. I've been with that man almost fifty years, and I can tell he's not himself. He's just so damn stubborn." She ran a hand through her glossy short salt-and-pepper locks. Her brown eyes, shaped the same as Eve's, held all the affection and concern she felt for her husband of forty-six years.

"So what are we going to do about him?" She took a seat next to her mother, looking across at the family photograph on the wall above the console table. The picture had been taken when she was about ten, around Christmastime. While part of her cringed at the wayward pigtail standing straight up on one side of her head, her heart smiled as she looked upon her father's face. In the photograph, he looked young, strong and steadfast—a broad-shouldered, sharp-dressed man lovingly embracing his wife and daughter. That was the man she knew and loved—not the tired, bent man she'd been seeing lately.

"I'm gonna keep after him. I intend to nag him until he gets himself checked out, no matter how long it takes. I've been putting up with him all these years, and I'm not giving him up now."

"Thanks, Mama. I think this software launch has put a lot of extra stress on Daddy's shoulders." She knew how excited her father was about the upcoming MyBusiness Sapphire product, an enthusiasm she shared. This would be the most comprehensive software suite they'd offered in years, and even though the launch was still a few months away, the product would be officially announced this week. After that, they'd have to contend with media attention and any possible competition from other firms, in addition to their already-packed launch preparation to-do list. "Everybody's been working so hard on it."

"I know. Times like this, I really enjoy my position as a silent board member. When y'all get to scrambling around, I don't have to take part in any of it."

She was familiar with her mother's point of view. For Louise, it was enough to be a part of Joseph's dream. She'd never had any interest in the intricate inner workings of the business, or in keeping up with ever-changing technological trends. When it came time to plan a party, though, Louise could be counted on to have everything in place. Celebrations were her forte.

"I guess I'll get on home, and get myself together for this week." She gave her mother a kiss on the cheek and stood. "Need help with anything before I go?"

Louise shook her head. "Maid will be in tomorrow, so go on home. I'll see you at the offices tomorrow."

She kissed her mother on the cheek again, then left, closing the front door behind her.

Outside, she climbed into her midsized SUV and started the engine. Alone in her car, she thought about the look that had come over her father's face when she mentioned taking over at FTI. She was the only heir to the business, and she'd worked hard alongside her parents to make it a success. Could he really doubt her abilities now, after everything she'd put into her work?

The city lights twinkled in the darkness, dotting the I-77 corridor like gems. Easing into the turn lane, she took a moment to take in the sight of the city. For a few seconds she admired the skyline. Then the light changed, and she turned her truck in the direction of her house.

Darius Winstead lifted the lid of his grill and turned over the four steaks on the grate. As he closed the lid, he took in the magnificent view from the patio of his vacation condo. Only a few hundred yards away, the Atlantic Ocean ebbed and flowed beneath a beautiful crystal-blue sky. The view was part of the reason he had bought his little Emerald Isle retreat, and he had plans to spend many more days here during his awesome retirement.

Just beyond the patio steps, his boys were competing in an epic game of volleyball, using the net he'd perched in the sand the day he'd bought the place. The three of them were his closest friends in the world; they all shared the same passion for sports and music—jazz in particular. They were grunting and shouting, and making serves and volleys as if they were professional athletes and the championship hung in the balance. The sight of it tickled him. If he weren't busy tending the grill, he'd be out there with them.

At twenty-eight, Darius had been a hot commodity in the tech world. Having graduated at the top of his class from North Carolina Agricultural and Technical State University with his master of science in information technology, he'd earned the opportunity to intern for his mentor, Joseph Franklin, at his software company. In a little less than four years, Darius had created the first smartphone operating system and sold it for $300 million. He then happily left the office politics and stuffy meetings behind. Even Rashad, Darius's closest friend, had called him a dumb ass for getting out of the software game when he did, but he had no regrets. He'd loved the creative side of software development, but the business side of things had pushed him far away. He didn't want to spend the rest of his life sitting in board meetings, going over expense reports and kowtowing to stockholders.

Now, at thirty-six, Darius spent his days doing the things he loved, and felt incredibly blessed to be able to do so. His time was his own, and that was just the way he wanted it. Just a few days after his official retirement party, he'd done the one thing he'd always wanted to do, the thing he'd been planning for months—form a band. He'd given up playing his bass during his early days in the tech business, but the day he'd picked it up again was as if he'd never put it down. His boys had been happy to join him in practicing, and once they'd felt comfortable with their skills, he'd started marketing the group. He and his friends were now the Queen City Gents, a jazz quartet that played regular local gigs and enjoyed an enthusiastic, mostly female following.

He watched Rashad McRae, his buddy since undergrad, take a flying leap that would have made any professional basketball player jealous as he returned the ball to Ken Yamada and Marco Alvarez on the other side. Rashad, who was the band's pianist and vocalist, had always imagined himself as the world's most powerful athlete. Darius wasn't a bit surprised that he'd chosen to play alone against their bandmates.

The grill's timer buzzed, and he opened the lid once again. He punctured the steaks with a fork to be sure they'd reached medium-well perfection. Satisfied, he grabbed his tongs and began moving the steaks to a ceramic platter. "Yo! Steaks are done!"

What had just moments ago been the most serious volleyball game ever played immediately came to a halt. The saxophonist, Marco Alvarez, captured the ball between his hands instead of returning it. All eyes turned toward Darius standing by the grill.

He made a gesture with his tongs, and the three men jogged up the sandy slope.

Rashad got there first, and leaned over the platter, inhaling deeply. "Smells good, man."

Darius jabbed him in the shoulder with the nonbusiness end of the tongs. "I know, but if you don't go wash your hands and quit breathing on my steaks, me and you are gonna fight."

Ken, toweling the sweat from his brow, chuckled. "He's right, Rashad. Don't let your hot breath overcook them." The laid-back drummer rarely spoke, but when he did, no one could predict what would come out of his mouth.

"Hardy har har." Rashad gave Darius a slap on the back before disappearing into the condo through the open French doors.

Darius shook his head. They were a crazy bunch, but

that was part of their charm. "That goes for all of you. Go wash them funky, sweaty hands before you come near my food. And put on some damn shirts while you're at it." The last thing he wanted was a bunch of sweaty shirtless dudes hanging around his culinary masterpiece.

While they went inside to do as they'd been told, he moved to the round table a few feet away from the grill. There, he'd set up the side items: grilled corn on the cob, baked beans and a Caesar salad. He placed the platter of steaks in the middle and set out the matching plates and the silverware. Then he lifted the lid of the cooler on the patio floor near the railing and pulled out four ice-cold beers.

By the time the guys returned, hands clean and chests covered, he was already sitting down, looking out over the water. They joined him around the table, loaded their plates and dug in.

Later, they were still reclining in their seats as the sun began to dip on the horizon. The bands of color seemed to go on forever, until they met with the rising waves. The sound of lapping water could be heard in the silence, along with the calls of a few seagulls.

Ken drained the last of his beer. "That's a beautiful sight, man."

Marco nodded, tossing his own empty bottle into the recycling bin. "Sure is."

"Yep. Wish I could stay longer, but I gotta go to work in the morning." Rashad stood up from the table, dragging his long dreadlocks into a ponytail at the base of his neck.

Darius groaned. "Aw, come on, y'all. You just gonna abandon a brother like that? How can you walk away from a sunset this magnificent?"

Marco snickered. "Easy. I just think about my mortgage."

"I work for the county, dude. I can't just not show up—my assistant will be happy to take my job in my absence."

Rashad worked as register of deeds for Mecklenburg County.

Darius turned to Ken. "What about you? You work for yourself. Don't you wanna hang out here for a few more days, and enjoy the place with me?"

"I would, man, but I didn't bring my computer." Ken offered a shrug. "No laptop, no work."

Marco leaned back in his chair, stretching his arms above his head. "I could be convinced to stay if you pay my mortgage."

"I'm with Marco. Pay my bills and I'll hang out with you as long as you want, D." Rashad cocked a thick eyebrow, waiting for his response.

Darius looked at his watch. "Um, never mind. Y'all better get out of here."

Chuckling, Marco got up. "Yeah, I thought so. We'll see you when you get back to Charlotte."

"Bye." Darius watched his buddies file into the condo to get their things. A short time later, he waved to them as their vehicles pulled out of the small lot in front of his condo.

Back inside his condo, he stripped out of his T-shirt and athletic shorts to climb into a hot shower. He stood there, enjoying the multiple jets of steamy water hitting his body from all angles. Once he'd dried off, he slipped into a pair of black boxers and stretched across his bed.

He mused on when he'd go back to Charlotte and decided he'd head back in a few days. He had a pet-sitter who looked after his golden retriever, Chance, so he'd just let her know when he was coming back. He would have loved to bring Chance along on the trip, but for some reason the dog hated Marco. Every time the dog got within ten feet of Mr. Costa Rico Suave, he growled and bared his teeth. What made it particularly weird was that Chance loved

Ken and Rashad, the maid, the mailman and just about any other person who came by the house. Knowing Chance would've freaked the hell out if he had to be near Marco over the weekend, he'd decided to leave the dog with the sitter. But when he traveled alone to his vacation place, Chance was always by his side.

The faint sounds of the water splashing against the shore reminded him that he'd left the patio doors open. He got up to close and lock them, and to crack the kitchen windows to allow the breeze to flow in, before sprawling across the bed once again. He reached behind him and grabbed the remote from the niche in his headboard.

He turned on the fifty-inch flat-screen television occupying a wall of the bedroom and flipped through the channels. He paused at one of those dating reality shows, where some guy in a suit was offering a flower to a squealing girl in a too-tight dress, and scoffed. It wasn't that he didn't believe in true love, but he damn sure didn't believe it could be found on some corny, scripted show. He couldn't figure out why those shows were so popular, but he guessed there had to be someone, somewhere, who really thought you could find love that way.

But he'd witnessed true love as a kid, so he knew it existed. He'd also seen what losing a true love could do to a man, when his mother had waltzed out the door, proclaiming her urge to sing was stronger than her maternal instincts. The day she'd left him and his father to fend for themselves was a day he couldn't forget, no matter how he tried. He'd seen his father, the man he looked up to and respected more than anyone in the world, reduced to tears that day. And even at a young age, he understood that his father was in pain, and that he never wanted to suffer that way.

Still, as he stretched out in the king-sized bed, he had

to admit that it might be nice to have a beautiful woman pressed up against him. He wrapped himself up in the crisp white sheets, which was as close as he was going to get to being held tonight. Sure, there were one or two ladies he could call on to warm his bed, but they didn't really meet his requirements. A woman he would fully let into his life would have to be intelligent, independent and graceful, but most of all, she'd have to be loyal. He required nothing less than total devotion from a woman, because he had no plans of ending up like his father; disrespected, disgraced and deserted.4

She would also have to accept the fact that he didn't have any desire to get married. To him, marriage represented nothing more than a legal contract, a piece of paper for the paperwork jockeys who worked down at the county courthouse with Rashad to sign off on. His parents had been married, but that hadn't stopped his mother from dishonoring her vows and basically spitting in his father's face when she left him. Why bother going through all the trouble of signing something, having a ceremony and putting on airs? None of that meant anything without a true commitment, and as far as he was concerned, there were already enough pretenses in the world.

The buzzing of his cell phone drew him back to reality. Reaching over to where it lay on the nightstand, he picked it up and looked at the display. The caller ID said Unknown, and he wondered who would be calling him on a Sunday night. Curious, he lightly touched the screen twice, answering the call and engaging the speakerphone.

"Hello?"

"Darius, is that you?" The female voice on the line sounded vaguely familiar, but he couldn't place it. Since he'd had the same cell phone number since grad school, there was really no telling who it was.

"Yes, who's this?" He stared at the phone's screen.

A few moments passed in silence, as if the woman were hesitant to reveal her identity. Finally, she took a deep breath. "This is Louise Franklin."

Chapter 2

Eve secured the crystal-beaded elastic around her low bun, then gave her reflection a final glance in the mirror. Satisfied with the look of her chocolate-brown pantsuit, gold jewelry and muted makeup, she flicked off the light on her vanity and rose to her feet. She was due at the monthly board meeting in less than an hour, and she knew she needed to get on the road in order to avoid the usual traffic in downtown Charlotte.

Within a few minutes, she'd made herself a cup of coffee and a bagel, grabbed her purse and briefcase, and flown out the door.

She strolled into the boardroom ten minutes before the meeting was set to begin. Glancing around the room, she could see that the seats around the long polished table were empty. Confused, she paused a moment, then backtracked to the open conference room door. There, a simple typed sign had been affixed to the glass. She read it—the board meeting had been postponed until 10 a.m. the next day. No explanation had been given.

She shrugged and returned to the corridor to get back on the elevator. The conference room was on the building's third floor, along with the employee lounge and the security offices. Her office was on the seventh floor, where the entire finance department was housed. She slipped into the car, jabbed the appropriate button on the elevator's panel and waited for the doors to close.

A half a second before the doors could meet, a hand wedged between them, making them part again. Her gaze followed the rather large hand up an arm clothed in a raven-black suit, the cuff of a cherry-red shirt visible at the wrist.

The doors opened fully, and in stepped the finest brother she'd ever had the pleasure of laying her eyes on. He wore a gray, red and black striped tie, a bold complement to the well-cut suit and crisp shirt. His hair was close cut, a neat fade. His chiseled, bronze-toned face was framed by a carefully trimmed beard and mustache. Two dark, mesmerizing eyes fixed on her, and two full lips turned up into a sinfully sexy smile. "Good morning."

For a moment, she just stood there, staring. The second he'd stepped into the space, he'd brought with him an intoxicating, masculine aroma. She picked up notes of sandalwood, eucalyptus and something else she couldn't quite identify.

Exhaling, she tried to form a verbal response, though her brain was a bit slow to cooperate. When she found her voice, she returned his greeting.

If he noticed how dumbfounded she looked, he didn't mention it. He gripped the strap of the attaché case slung over his shoulder with one hand, and used his free hand to press the button for the eighth floor. "Good, you're already going up. Wouldn't want to keep a lovely lady like yourself from any important appointments."

She tried to stop herself, but before she knew it, her tongue darted out to wet her bottom lip. Damn, this man was fine. So fine she could barely think. Looking at him was like looking at the sun—awfully pretty, but it sure did make your eyes hurt. Rather than put her foot in her mouth, she simply smiled and nodded.

No one said anything for the few moments they shared the elevator car. She was perfectly fine with pressing her back into the corner, gripping the handrail and staring at his back. The dark suit fit him so well it must have been custom-made. Despite her father's efforts to hire on as many people of color as possible, there just weren't that many brothers working at FTI. That was why a well-dressed brother like him stood out, or at least that was what she told herself.

As the automated voice announced their arrival at the seventh floor, she extricated herself from the corner and prepared to get off. The doors opened, and she attempted to ease by him without making eye contact.

She succeeded in doing that, but didn't manage to evade him entirely. As he stuck his arm out to make sure the doors didn't shut on her, his hand brushed against her arm. She glanced back, and found his smiling eyes on her.

"Have a great day, beautiful." He gave her a wink.

She stepped back, out into the hallway, and the elevator doors closed. Just like that, Mr. Sexy Mystery Man was gone. That disappointed her a bit, but at least she could think straight now that he'd taken his sexiness and delicious scent elsewhere.

Swiveling to her right, she strode down the hall toward her corner office. By now, her secretary should have some coffee made—maybe a kick of caffeine would help her concentrate on her work and put the fine, nameless brother out of her mind.

Stepping into her custom-designed office put a smile on her face, as it did most days. Her parents had given her free reign to decorate the office in any manner she liked. She'd chosen a calming color palette of cream and periwinkle. The brocade-textured wallpaper, shelving units and furniture all reflected her tastes. She'd had light oak hardwood floors put in, and covered them with soft throw rugs in muted shades of blue. The theme started in the reception area, and carried through her personal office and washroom.

In the reception area, she found Mimi Chin, her secretary, stationed at her desk. After they'd exchanged greetings, Eve made a beeline for the coffeepot. The smell of the brew met her before she was fully in the room, and she noticed it was stronger than what she usually drank. Picking up the pot, she turned toward Mimi. "What's this?"

"French roast. I try to make something with a little more gusto on board-meeting days." Mimi was typing furiously on her keyboard, and didn't look up.

"Thanks." Even though the board meeting had been delayed, she could still use the kick to get her going.

As she headed toward the door to her private office, her phone buzzed. Removing it from the outer pocket of her leather hobo, she looked at the screen.

It was a text from Lina. Opening it, she found a picture attached of Lina and two of their girlfriends in bathing suits, standing on the beach. The message read, Girl, you missed it!

She smiled, shaking her head. Lina was about as straitlaced as could be when it came to her work as an attorney specializing in employment law. But when Lina cut loose, she did it like she was doing it for TV. She spent another moment looking at the picture, and was about to close it and tuck her phone away when she noticed something in the background.

Or rather, someone.

Standing behind her friends, mere feet away, was a handsome man, wearing nothing but a pair of bright blue swim trunks and a silver chain. The photo had been taken with him in midair, smacking a volleyball over the net.

His muscled arms and chest glistened in the sunlight as he hovered a couple of inches off the ground. Dark shades obscured his eyes, but the distinctive facial hair was a dead giveaway.

The man in the picture was the same man who'd stolen her breath when he stepped into her elevator car.

Fingers laced together, Darius tucked his hands behind his head. He'd been told to make himself comfortable in the swanky eighth-floor office he'd been directed to, and was taking those instructions to heart. The burgundy chair he sat in was so comfortable he never wanted to get up. He could feel his butt sinking into the fabric, and sighed with pleasure. There was nothing like a comfortable chair to put him in a good mood. As a bonus, the chair faced a wall made entirely of glass, giving him an impressive view of the Queen City's lush skyline beneath a sun-filled sky.

It had been years since he'd been in this building, let alone this office. Back then, he'd been fresh out of school and eager to learn everything he could about software development. His passion for innovation had been at its zenith. There was no way he could have guessed that his enthusiasm for designing programs would be extinguished by the rigors of the business side of things. The day he'd graduated, he thought he'd spend his life in the field. But in reality, he'd spent less than ten years in the industry before he became burned out.

His thoughts drifted to the lovely lady he'd been on the elevator with earlier. She was taller than most of the women he ran into, though still nowhere near his six-foot-three-inch frame. Aside from that, she had a figure that could only be described as voluptuous—full breasts, a tapered waist and round hips, all encased in a little brown pantsuit. While the suit was very professional and not at all revealing, it did nothing to hide her shape and he was glad of it. He clearly recalled the way her glossy, straight brown hair was tucked into a demure looking bun. It looked so soft, he'd had to shove his hands in his pockets to keep from touching it. But the thing about her that really got his blood flowing was her lips—plump, pouty, perfect. She'd painted them with some kind of shimmery raspberry-colored gloss that made them look incredibly tempting. If his boys had been in the elevator with him, they'd probably have come to blows over who would get to ask her out.

Behind him, the double doors of the office opened, then closed again, but he didn't turn around. He was too busy enjoying the view.

"Sorry to keep you waiting, Darius." Joseph Franklin marched across the room to engulf Darius in a paternal embrace. Then he took a seat behind the big desk between Darius's comfy chair and the wall of windows. "What has it been, three or four years since I've seen you? How have you been?"

"Yeah, it's been about that long. I've been great. Retirement suits me quite nicely." Taking in the sight of his mentor, he could see the older man had changed a lot since he'd last seen him. His shoulders slumped just a bit, his kind face had many new lines and his once dark hair had gone gray. In a word, Franklin looked tired. "How about you?"

"Busy, but good." Franklin leaned back in the leather executive chair, running his fingertips through his graying beard.

Never one for small talk, Darius thought it prudent to proceed with the matter at hand. "I was surprised to hear from Mrs. Franklin the other night. I talked to her for a little while, but just so I'm clear, what is it you need me to do?"

Joseph hesitated for a moment, then sighed. "I know

you're enjoying your leisure, but I could really use your expertise here at FTI."

"Okay. So you want me on a freelance basis? Some consulting?" He would do what he could to help the older man out. After all, he'd gotten his start in the tech world under Franklin's watchful tutelage.

"The role would be a little more involved than consulting, Darius."

Darius was becoming more and more impatient to find out what exactly Franklin wanted. He leaned forward in his seat. "What are you really asking me for, Mr. Franklin?"

"Why so formal? Call me Joe." A ghost of a smile crossed his face.

His eyebrow hitched up. "Ok, Joe, what are we really talking about here?"

Joseph leaned forward, braced his arms on the surface of the big desk. "Darius, I'd like you to take over as CEO."

Darius blinked, then focused on Franklin's face again. Had he heard what he thought he heard? "Excuse me?"

"This isn't easy for me to ask of you, Darius."

He raised his hand, scratched his chin. His first instinct was to say no. All he wanted to do was extract his butt from the seductive chair, leave the building and get back in his car so he could go home and practice for his band's next gig. His time was his own now, and that was just the way he liked it. No clock to punch, no boss to answer to and the freedom to pursue his own interests, any way he saw fit. He was living the life most people dreamed of, and at a very young age. He'd received plenty of offers and requests to come back to the tech business since he'd gone into retirement, but this time was different. If it hadn't been for Franklin, he might never have had the means to take his retirement when he did. How could he flatly turn down the man who'd given him his first shot in this game? The answer was simple: he couldn't.

Still, there was another contingency here, one that needed to be discussed. "What about your daughter? I assumed she'd be the one to take over things here when you retired."

Franklin rose from his chair, easing toward the windows. His eyes seemed focused on the goings-on outside as he spoke. "So did I. But she isn't ready quite yet." His flat tone conveyed a measure of disappointment.

Having never met Franklin's daughter, he didn't know what her skill set was. During the time he'd been at FTI, she'd been in college and studying abroad. She might be less than prepared in Franklin's eyes, but he found the old man's assessment a little blunt. "Come on now, Joe. Any daughter of yours has got to be bright enough to learn the ropes, with time and training."

He shook his head, still gazing out the window. "True, but time is a luxury I don't have anymore. I waited too long to train her the way I should have—I thought she would've caught on a bit faster on her own. Now..." He stroked a hand over his head, but didn't complete the statement.

A few moments passed in silence before Darius spoke. "Is there something else I need to know?"

"My health isn't at its best, Darius. I'm going in for some tests this week, because if I don't, my wife won't give me a moment's peace. I really don't know what the doctor is going to tell me, but I know I'm not getting any younger."

"And there's no one you could promote from within the company ranks?"

Franklin shook his head. "I believe what FTI really needs is a cutting-edge, youthful approach. Besides, you've got the brightest technological mind to ever grace the halls of this building."

"I appreciate that." He could see where this was headed. Clasping his hands together, he took a moment to collect his thoughts. There was nothing interfering with his ability to do what Franklin was asking of him, though taking the job might interfere with his involvement with the Gents. Undeniably, he owed this man a debt of thanks for the role he'd played in starting his career. "If you really feel you need me, I'll do it. But how does your daughter feel about all of this?" He searched his memory banks, but couldn't recall her name.

For several seconds, the only sounds Darius heard were the ringing phones and low conversation beyond the doors of the private office. He folded his arms and waited, wondering what he'd gotten himself into. "Joe?"

"I'm not entirely sure. We haven't discussed it with her yet. Either way, she's not ready and you're the one I want."

Darius rolled his eyes, letting loose an exasperated sigh. "Joe, we both know that if she doesn't agree with our little arrangement, she's likely going to make my job very difficult."

The old man returned to his desk, leaned over it and made eye contact with him. "Look, I may be uncertain of Eve's leadership ability, but I don't doubt her professionalism. So give her a chance before you make assumptions about her, all right?"

So that was her name. Picking up on the defensive edge in Franklin's tone, he shrugged. "Fair enough." His mentor seemed pretty torn about this whole thing—going from saying his daughter wasn't ready to assume command, to praising her professionalism in a matter of minutes. He glanced at his watch. "So, what's the salary? And is this a temporary position?"

"I'm not sure of the duration—that depends on Eve, and

how soon she can be groomed. You'll get a competitive salary, full benefits and vacation time, of course."

It was a reasonable compensation offer, perhaps even a bit more than he warranted. "Sounds good." He reached across the table to shake hands with his mentor. "I'll do the best job I can, Joe."

"I have no doubt of that." Franklin stood, gesturing toward the door. "I won't hold you up all day, but we do have a board meeting tomorrow at ten. I'd like you to be there, so I can introduce you to everyone."

"I'll be here."

Pondering the many possibilities of this new venture, Darius bid his mentor goodbye and slipped out of the large office, shutting the door behind him.

Chapter 3

Eve joined her parents in the sunroom, carrying the tray of Italian fare she'd ordered for dinner. Her mother had thrown open a few of the windows, letting the late-summer breeze blow through the room. Setting the tray down on the mosaic dining table, she began taking the lids off the containers. "I got some primavera for you, Daddy, chicken Parmesan for you, Mama, and a little baked ziti for me." While she considered herself a woman of many talents, cooking wasn't one of them. Her parents were well aware of her lack of culinary skills, so they weren't surprised when she'd brought over the food prepared by her favorite private chef, Alfonzo. Some of the wealthiest families in the area could be counted among his clients.

She sat down and reached for the pitcher of iced tea on the table—the one thing she had made herself—and filled her glass. She was about to take a sip when she stopped, holding the glass in midtip. Her mother and father were staring at her, both with odd looks on their faces. "What's the problem? Why are you guys staring at me like that?"

No answer. Instead, her parents' gazes shifted, until they were looking at each other.

"Mama?"

Louise sighed.

Her brow furrowing, she turned to her father. "Daddy? What in the world is going on?"

Joseph picked up his glass, took a long draw of tea. "Well, baby, we have some news."

"Okay. What is it?" She rested her palms on the table, and waited.

"First, you'll be glad to know I made a doctor's appointment. I'm going in on Friday for a whole slew of tests."

She nodded, offering a smile. "That is good news. But I feel like there's something else."

Louise spoke up. "There is. Your father is retiring, finally."

Eve reached across the table to grasp his hand. When she did, she found it to be a bit cool and clammy. "I'm proud of you for putting your health first, Daddy. And I want you to know I'm going to make you proud. I'll lead FTI as honorably as you have."

He cleared his throat, his gaze drifting away from hers.

Something wasn't right.

She felt the tension in the room begin to creep into her shoulders and neck. Still holding his hands, she stared at him. "Daddy, what is it you're not saying?"

He looked at her, but only briefly. Then he cast his eyes down again, as if studying the carpet beneath his slipper-clad feet. "Lord. I didn't think this would be so hard."

Now she was worried. Her pulse sped up, her mouth went dry. What were they keeping from her? "Will somebody please tell me what is going on?"

"I'm sorry, baby. So sorry." He had yet to look up,

This was getting pretty disconcerting. First they'd stared at her, now her father was taking evasive maneuvers to avoid looking at her, and apologizing on top of that? Something had to give.

The silence grew thick, palpable. Her brow creasing into a frown, she looked to her mother for an explanation.

"Your father and I discussed it, and we don't feel you're quite ready for the CEO position, at least not yet." Her mother's eyes were damp, and held what appeared to be sympathy.

The words hit her like a handful of crushed ice to the face. She jerked back in her seat, drew her hand away from her father's. "What do you mean, I'm not ready? I've been with FTI my whole professional life—everything I've done was in preparation for this day."

"I know, Eve," her father said. "But you're still in need of a bit more training in the operations of the company. When you're ready, the job is yours." He reached for his glass of tea.

This was the last thing she'd expected to hear. She'd been watching her father run FTI all her life. Some of her earliest memories were of toddling around the Franklin Technologies building and sitting in her father's big chair, coloring on scrap paper. Aside from that, she held an MBA with honors and had been closely studying the inner workings of the company for the past several years. She worked hard every day at the top of the finance department, so how could they think she wasn't ready? "Who's going to take over now, until I'm 'ready'?" She emphasized the last word, struggling to remain respectful to her parents despite the negative emotions swirling inside her.

"He's an old friend, and a brilliant technologist. He's coming out of retirement to help out, until you're ready." He finally made eye contact with her. "I still have every faith in your abilities, Eve. But for now, I feel this is the best way to proceed."

That drew a bitter chuckle from her lips. So, an old man, and an outsider, was coming into their family business and denying her the chance to run the company? "Seriously, Daddy? You'd rather turn things over to a senior citizen than give me a chance to prove myself?"

He shook his head. "I didn't say he was old, just that he was an old friend. You'll meet him at tomorrow's board meeting. We'll make the official announcement then."

"What if I never meet your standards? Will this person get to keep the job, then?"

He pursed his lips. "That's pretty unlikely, Eve."

Anger and hurt coursed through her veins. Based on what she was hearing, her opinion on the matter didn't count, it had already been decided. She looked down at her untouched pasta. While the delicious aroma of garlic, tomato sauce and cheese filled her nostrils, she found she'd lost her appetite. Pushing back from the table, she stood.

"Don't run off, Eve. Stay and enjoy dinner. We'll talk this through." Her mother's eyes pleaded with her.

"Sorry, Mama. I'm not hungry anymore. Besides, it doesn't look like there's anything to talk about. I'll see you tomorrow morning." Tears stung the corners of her eyes. All she wanted to do was get out of there before they saw her cry. Snatching her cardigan from the back of the chair, she shrugged into it.

Joseph rose to his feet. "Eve, I expect you to be professional about all this. I haven't lost faith in you, baby. Once you learn how to handle the shareholders, the public relations end and a few other things, you'll be ready. You've got to understand…"

Her eyes locked with his, she ignored the tears streaming down her cheek. "I'm sorry, Daddy, but I don't understand any of this."

Before anyone could say another word, she bolted from the room. Tears blinded her path, but she swiped them away as she grabbed her purse and keys from the stone table near the front door.

With her mother calling her name, she flung open the door and ran out, slamming it behind her.

When Eve walked into the boardroom Tuesday morning, the space was alive with conversation. Most of the seats around the table were full, and as she pulled out her chair to the right of her father's seat at the head of the table, she exchanged greetings with the other executives and board members present. In a way, this was just like any of the other board meetings she attended on a monthly basis. She knew there would be departmental reports, motions and a matter of dull details to hash out. But today's meeting would be different, and she wasn't sure how she'd react when the time came to make the announcement.

Last night, she'd cried herself to sleep. Today, however, she would do her best to honor her father's request and be professional. The die had been cast, and there was no need of her making a fool of herself in front of everyone. No matter how hard it was, she was going to try to keep her emotions in check, at least until she was alone.

The room continued to fill with people as 10 a.m. approached. Louise came in, sat across from her in the chair to the left of her father's seat and offered a small smile. Her mother reached across the table's polished surface and grasped her hand. Eve said nothing, but offered a nod and a small smile of her own in return.

At two minutes till, her father finally strode in. Another man entered the room on his heels, and she felt a charge in the air. The atmosphere changed around her as a familiar scent filled her nostrils.

Her eyes traveled up the body of the man accompanying her father. His muscular frame was draped in a well-fitting gray suit, soft blue shirt and deep blue tie. Her gaze went higher, to meet the man's face.

The dark eyes met hers, and recognition lit them almost immediately.

Shit!

Her mind registered who he was: the shirtless brother in the background of the picture Lina had texted her. Before she could stop herself, she said aloud, "Oh my God, it's the elevator and volleyball guy..."

All eyes turned on her, including the sexy ones belonging to the brother in the gray suit.

He'd heard her.

She closed her eyes, and wished the floor would open up and swallow her.

What is she talking about?

Darius blinked, held his eyes closed for a moment, then opened them again.

But that didn't change anything. The beautiful woman he'd seen on the elevator yesterday was still there, wide-eyed.

Today she wore a navy blue sheath dress that just grazed her knees. He found he much preferred it to yesterday's pantsuit, as this getup allowed him an unobstructed view of her long, silky-looking brown legs.

Thinking he should respond to what she'd said, he dragged his eyes upward, toward her face. "I'm sorry, but I can't say I've ever played volleyball in an elevator." It was a nonsense response to match the nonsense statement, and he hoped it would break the tension hanging between them.

She appeared mortified, her cheeks filled with red. She dipped her head, lay a graceful hand over her brow, as if doing her best to disappear. "That didn't come out right."

Aware of the watching eyes of everyone present, he offered an easy chuckle. "Apparently."

A few laughs sounded around the table.

Someone even made a comment about how the size of an elevator simply wasn't conducive to a good volleyball game.

"Unless we're talking about a handheld game," someone else interjected.

To him, they were just disembodied voices in a crowded room. His eyes stayed on the pretty lady who'd captured his attention the previous day. The one who was now doing her best to avoid looking at him. "It's all right to misspeak now and then, you know."

She looked up at him, her face tight, the brown eyes narrowed. "Forget what I said. What I mean is, I've seen you before."

"How could I forget?" He smiled at her, coming a little closer to her seat, and taking her hand. "It's nice to see you again, Miss..."

Her hand trembled, and as she tilted her face to look at him, a silken lock of her upswept hair fell into her face. He found the sight captivating.

Someone cleared their throat. "I see you've met my daughter, Eve."

He jerked his head around, and saw Franklin there, looking on. Releasing her hand, he studied his mentor, whose face was unreadable. "This is your daughter?"

Franklin nodded in response.

Turning back to her, he met her curious eyes. "Pleased to meet you, again, Miss Franklin. I'm Darius Winstead—an old friend of your father's."

In a moment, her expression changed from curiosity to anger. Her lovely brows furrowed, her sweet little painted mouth twisted into a scowl. In an outraged whisper, she said, "You! You're the old friend?"

Not wanting to rile her any further, he stepped back. "Yes, I guess I am."

She opened her mouth, then closed it again, as if becoming aware of the other people in the room. Blowing out a loud sigh, she folded her arms over her chest and turned toward the center of the table. She was obviously angry about something. But rather than say anything else, and risk a shouting match with her in front of the people he would soon lead, he rounded the table and took a seat in an empty leather chair across from her. She cut her eyes at him, a brief gesture that communicated her desire to either slap him, or let the air out of his tires, or both. He couldn't tell and he didn't want to find out.

So, the gorgeous woman from the elevator was the old man's daughter. He never would have guessed it, having only seen pictures of her as a child scattered around Franklin's office. What really upset him, though, was the way she reacted when he'd introduced himself. Why was she so annoyed that he called her father a friend?

Franklin stood behind the chair at the head of the table, and called the meeting to order. Soon the old man had called on the board secretary to read aloud the minutes of the last meeting. Darius knew he should probably pay attention to what was being said, but this was the part of business that bored him into a coma-like state. When he looked across the table at a tight-faced Eve, he saw her drumming the eraser end of a sharpened pencil on the tabletop. At least he wasn't the only person struggling to stay awake.

To keep his eyelids from growing any heavier, he took a moment to look around the room. It was a very modern space, with soft gray walls and matching carpet. One wall was similar to the one in Franklin's office, all glass, and looked out onto Trade Street. The other three walls were hung with framed magazine and newspaper articles about FTI, as well as a few pieces of colorful abstract art. The table they were sitting around was long and rectangular, made of glossy polished mahogany or some other dark wood. The twenty or so people present were all sitting in chairs the same shade of dark brown leather, with padded armrests. He shifted in his seat. It wasn't as comfy as the memory foam one upstairs, but the slight discomfort might be just enough to keep him awake.

He heard Franklin call his daughter's name and ask her to summarize the past month's financial reports. She stood, tugging at the hem of the sheath dress. An aide walked over and turned on the projector set up in front of the room's only blank wall. As the aide operated a laptop slide show, Eve pushed the wayward lock of hair away from her face and began to speak. Angling herself away from him and facing more toward her father, she spoke about profits and losses, overhead and the other particulars of the company budget with confidence. Watching her, it was pretty obvious she knew what she was talking about, and was likely damn good at her job. Why was Franklin so sure she wasn't ready for the position of CEO? From where he sat, she seemed altogether capable and intelligent.

Once the slide show and her presentation came to an end, she sat down again. Impressed with both her body itself and her body of knowledge, Darius kept his eyes on her for the rest of the meeting.

Finally, mercifully, the meeting came to an end. Most of the people in the room filtered out, but Darius remained, along with Franklin and his daughter. The old man, who'd stood as the board members exited, sat down again. Eve remained in her seat, and they both looked in his direction. Taking the hint, he got up and moved down to the seat Mrs. Franklin had been occupying, with the old man between them.

Franklin started. “Eve, I…”

She cut him off. “Please excuse me, Daddy, but I would really like to know what qualifies your so-called ‘old friend’ to run this company. What kind of experience does he have that I don’t?” She leaned forward, her elbows resting on the table.

Darius heard the challenge in her voice. “Straight to the point, I see. I like that.”

She pursed her lips. “Then why don’t you answer my question, Mr. Winstead?”

So it’s like that. She was going to get formal with him, condescendingly. That was fine. He liked a little spark of excitement in his life. If she wanted to play the game that way, he had no qualms about laying it all out on the table. He sat back in his chair, laced his fingers in front of him. “Please, call me Darius. As for my qualifications, I hold a bachelor of science in computer science, and an MBA as well as a master’s in information technologies. I interned here at FTI in the nineties, owned my own software company, Winstead Development, in the early two-thousands. I invented the first smartphone operating system, sold it and for the past six years I’ve been enjoying a pretty sweet retirement.” He cocked his head to one side. “Does that answer your question?”

Silence.

Her dark lashes fluttered in time with her rapid blinking, the surprise evident on her face. Her cherry-red lips hung just slightly open.

Franklin looked on without a word, although the slight upturn of his mouth gave away his amusement.

The room grew so quiet, he could hear her breathing.

For a moment, he watched the rise and fall of her chest as she leaned close over the tabletop.

"Ms. Franklin? Have I sufficiently satisfied your curiosity?" He flexed his fingers.

Closing her mouth, she swallowed. Making direct eye contact with him, she nodded. "Yes, Mr. Winstead. I'd say you have." She sat up, and pressed her back against the chair's tall backrest.

Franklin pulled a handkerchief from an inner pocket of his sport jacket, dabbed at the moisture gathering on his brow. "Good. Now I feel I can leave you two alone to get acquainted." He stood, retrieved his briefcase from the floor and made his way toward the open door. "You two play nice." With that, he exited.

Darius looked across the table at his new colleague. She'd let her head fall back against the top of the backrest, her eyes focused on the ceiling tiles above them. She used her feet to swivel the chair a few degrees left, then a few degrees right.

He watched her for a few moments. Something was obviously on her mind, but with the bit of tension still hanging in the air, he didn't know if he should ask.

But finally curiosity got the better of him. "Do you think we can get along, Ms. Franklin? Can we keep this professional?" Before the last word left his lips, he knew it was going to be mighty hard to keep things that way with her. She was a beauty, full of fire and grace, like a Miles Davis recording.

She straightened, looked at him with a slight frown. "Don't worry. Professionalism is my area of expertise. You are standing between me and my destiny, but I'm not petty."

He circled the table until he was standing next to her chair. "I don't doubt it, but that's not what I meant."

Her expression changed, and she looked away. "I don't know what you're talking about, then."

"Sure you do. From the moment I stepped into that elevator with you yesterday, you've been on my mind." He knew he was taking a risk, but he couldn't resist. With his fingertips, he touched the edge of her hairline, brushing back the hair that had fallen over her forehead once again. It was just as soft to his touch as he'd imagined it would be. "There's something between us. Something incredible."

The smallest of sighs slipped from her lips, and she clamped a hand over her mouth. Shifting in her seat to draw away from his touch, she shook her head. "Let's not even go down that road."

He wasn't about to let Ms. Sassy Mouth squirm her way out of this one. "Are you trying to tell me you don't feel it?" He touched her again, this time brushing his fingertips against her cheek.

The brief contact was enough to get her to shift again, then stand. When she did, her body was mere centimeters from his. "It doesn't matter. I don't date people I work with, Mr. Winstead."

He smiled. Her mouth was telling him what she didn't do, but what she hadn't said resonated with him even more. She hadn't denied her attraction to him, she'd only dismissed it as irrelevant. He eased nearer to her, closing the gap between them until his chest grazed hers. "I can't just ignore how you make me feel. But call me Darius, and we can agree to disagree on this."

"We both know that if I called you by your first name, I'd be encouraging you." She raised her eyes to meet his, and for a moment, he saw the passion there. Her lips parted, as if she had more to say.

Of their own accord, his fingertips found the softness of her cheek once more. Whatever she was going to say next was muffled as he pressed his lips against hers. The kiss was short, fleeting, but unbearably sweet. Her mouth was softer and more intoxicating than anything he'd ever encountered. When she pulled away, he could feel the buttery remnants clinging to his lips—traces of her cherry lipstick left behind.

In the aftermath, she took a step back but didn't break eye contact with him. To his mind, she looked conflicted, as if she couldn't decide what to do or say next.

"Have a good day, Darius."

The soft-spoken words still hanging in the air, she gathered her purse and slipped from the room.

Chapter 4

Around eight that evening, Eve pulled her car into a VIP parking space at the Charlotte Westin. Bar 10, a favorite haunt of Eve, Lina and their book club buddies, dominated the first floor of the hotel. Ophelia, Cara and Tammy weren't joining them tonight, and she was looking forward to some one-on-one time with her closest friend.

She'd spent the entire crosstown drive replaying her encounter with Darius. There was something about him that made her common sense drain away. How could she have let herself be drawn in by his good looks and smooth talk? She knew better than to start anything with him, regardless of the fact that his good looks made her eyes sting. Yet she'd let him kiss her. She'd had ample time and the opportunity to stop him but she hadn't. She brought her fingertips to her mouth, remembering what it felt like to have his lips crushed against her own. The memory of his kiss was vivid, intoxicating...and she could never let it happen again.

Realizing she still sat in her car, she unbuckled her seat belt, gathered her keys and purse, and hopped out. The sun hung low on the horizon, almost done with its daily trip across the sky. Up and down College Street, pedestrians strolled by, cars whizzed past and the trees lining the sidewalk swayed in the evening breeze. The beauty of the city wasn't lost on her, but on days like this it took a bit of extra effort to put her own thoughts aside long enough to enjoy it. Perching her sunglasses on top of her head, she entered the hotel in her favorite pair of pearl-white stilettos and sauntered toward the bar. Her eyes scanned the room for her friend.

The atmosphere at Bar 10 made it the perfect place for Eve and her gal pals to hold court. The large windowed wall facing the street gave a beautiful view of the Queen City and its residents coming and going; the comfortable furniture, tasteful decor and accommodating staff all conspired to create an inviting, relaxing destination at the end of a hard day.

Lina sat near the left side of the bar, in a caramel suede armchair beneath the large window that composed the entire wall. Eve spotted her easily, sitting crossed legged on the chair, wearing her typical evening attire: a silver sequined halter top and black pencil skirt with silver stilettos. A black clutch lay on the floor at her feet. Engrossed in the latest issue of *Essence* magazine on her lap, she didn't notice Eve until she slipped into the chair next to her.

"Hey, Eve," Lina said, looking up from the magazine. "Well, even after surviving another day as a sista in corporate America, you look good, girl." She glanced out the window, spotting Eve's car sitting in the lot. "Ready to trade war stories?"

Eve smiled, trying to push away her introspective mood. "Sure. We'll see who had the most interesting day."

"So." Lina crossed her long legs. "What are you drinking?"

To answer her question, Eve flagged down a passing waiter. "Could I get a frozen cosmo, please?"

"And I'll have a Midori Sour," Lina added.

"Coming right up, ladies." The waiter disappeared behind the bar to place their order.

With an exaggerated sigh, Eve dropped her black leather designer bag onto the nearby cocktail table and sank back into her chair. "Well, get ready to hear my latest horror story."

"Spill it."

"Well, you know I had to sit through one of those dull-as-hell board meetings this morning, but I do that every month. Today, it was even worse because I met the guy who's taking my job."

Lina's expression conveyed her empathy. "I know you were crushed when your parents told you."

She shook her head, feeling her emotions rise just thinking about it. "It amazes me that they didn't even talk to me about it before they made their decision. I've been training my whole life for this, and now I'm losing out, just because they doubt my abilities." She knew her parents hadn't set out to hurt her, but knowing that they didn't believe in her at such a critical time was a truly painful thing to accept.

"We both know you're fully capable of running FTI. Don't worry, they'll come around." Lina placed a comforting hand on her shoulder. "What's this new guy like, anyway? Isn't he a friend of your dad's?"

"Yes." She rolled her eyes, thinking back. "Here I was expecting a baby boomer but the brother who walked in couldn't be more than thirty-five. So, of course, I'm wondering what a guy this young could possibly have over me, in terms of business acumen and all that."

Lina's brow hitched up. "Really? So what does he have?"

She recalled the things Darius had said to her when he'd introduced himself. "He's young, but experienced. He's educated, has owned a software business previously and apparently invented the first smartphone operating system before retiring a few years ago."

"Wow. Sounds impressive."

She sighed. "Well, he must hear that a lot. This man is so damn arrogant. I mean, he just walked up in there as if he was just crowned king."

Lina didn't say anything, but rested her chin in her hands.

"It gets worse. This isn't the first time I met him." She grabbed her purse and unzipped the outside compartment, fishing out her phone. "Remember the guy in the elevator the other day, the one I told you about?"

"Oh, yeah. You said he was in the picture I sent you from our girl's weekend at Emerald Isle." Lina pulled her own phone out of her skirt pocket. "Wait, do you mean the new CEO is Elevator Volleyball Guy?"

She nodded. "Yes, and I was so shocked I said that out loud and completely embarrassed myself."

Her friend looked thoughtful for a moment, as if her lawyer mind was working a case. Then, she asked, "If this is the same brother in the picture, with the washboard abs..." She sucked air through her teeth. "Girl, I don't know how you managed not to lay hands on the brother."

Eve frowned, placed a hand to her forehead. "Well... I...I mean, we..."

Lina slid forward until she was perched on the edge of her seat. "Whatever it is, you better tell me."

She hesitated for a moment, then caved to the scrutiny. "He hung around after the meeting. He boldly pointed out that he was attracted to me, and then...kissed me. I didn't stop him, even though I could have." Seeing the glint of mischief in her friend's eyes, she shook her head. "No, Lina. Don't start."

"As an attorney, I can tell you that if there's an antifraternization policy on the books at FTI, you'd better steer clear of him." Lina leaned back in her chair. "As your girlfriend, though, I'd say you'd better take that stallion for a long ride, honey."

Eve clamped a hand over her mouth to cover the peals of laughter, but they escaped, anyway. "Lina! You're outrageous." She found herself wondering if the company had such a policy, then quickly pushed the thought away. "It doesn't matter if we have a policy against it or not. I'm not the type who can date someone I work with. It would ruin my focus."

"Whatever. Like lusting after this dude is going to make you razor sharp." She winked.

"I'm done talking about this with you, Lina. Now it's time you told me about your drama." She scanned the room, wondering where the waiter was with their drinks. All this talk about Darius had her craving the alcoholic beverage.

Lina scoffed. "You're complaining that a good-looking man is after you. I'm not getting any play at all. Girl, I haven't been on a date in two months." She held up her forefinger and middle finger to emphasize her statement. "Two months! I'm about to go straight up crazy."

"And what's your excuse? You don't meet any successful, eligible men in the world of law?"

She rolled her eyes. "No, that's not it. Everywhere I turn, there's some fine man in a suit. Judges, other lawyers, that fine-ass bailiff down at the courthouse…" Her words trailed off, and she appeared to be imagining said bailiff in her mind's eye. "But unlike you, Ms. Executive, I have to be very careful not to violate ethics codes."

"I could understand that. But is there really a law keeping you from getting busy with the bailiff?"

"Shut up!" Lina shouted with mock irritation, tossing one of her silver stilettos at Eve in a playful manner.

At that moment, the waiter approached with their drinks. After almost dropping the tray down on the cocktail table between their two chairs, he left. Eve and Lina continued giggling as he moved away, and then went back to gossiping.

Darius strolled into Tibbs Music and More, maneuvering the large protective case holding his bass around until it was safely inside the store. He let the door swing shut behind him and made his way over to the counter. As he walked, he bopped his head to the strains of Esperanza Spalding's "Little Fly," which played on the store's PA system. He enjoyed the music of the young bassist, and also found her wild mane of curls to be very sexy.

Behind the counter, Murphy Tibbs stood, rifling through a box of receipts. "Hey there, Darius. Time for Miss Molly's tuning and maintenance, eh?"

He nodded as he lifted the case up and set it carefully on the counter. "Sure is, and you know I don't trust anybody with her but you, Murph." And that was the truth. Miss Molly was a G. B. Rogeri upright bass, a copy of an instrument originally played by its famous Italian namesake. The bass was top quality, fashioned of hand-planed, hand-varnished maple and spruce. Though Miss Molly was a bit deeper than the average bass, she was an absolute dream to set up and play on stage, and she still fit into a standard case. The one he'd purchased for her, made of Kevlar, had set him back two grand on top of Miss Molly's $4,500 purchase price. But when he was on stage, jamming with the band and getting lost in the magic of the music, he knew it was money well spent.

"I'm sure you know I value that trust." Murphy slid the

case closer to himself, then carefully moved it to the floor behind the counter. "I'll have her ready for you bright and early tomorrow morning. Stop back in around nine."

Darius took his wallet out from the pocket of his khaki trousers and extracted six twenty dollar bills. "Thanks a lot, Murph. See you tomorrow." After passing the money to the shopkeeper, he turned around and left the store.

Outside, a few clouds passed over, temporarily dimming the bright sunlight streaming from above. He strode to his car, parked a few feet from the door of Tibbs, and slipped inside. Soon he eased his car into the traffic, joining the citizens of Charlotte rushing around to grab their lunch before their breaks expired.

As he sat at a red light, he pondered his current situation. He had a standing appointment, every second Thursday of the month, to drop Miss Molly off for maintenance and tuning. Other than that, Saturday basketball games and band practice, and the Gents' regular twice monthly gig at the Blue Lounge, he had no other demands placed on his time. Now, however, that was all about to change. Accepting the job as CEO at Franklin Technologies meant doing a favor for his old mentor, but it also meant giving up a lot of the freedom he'd come to enjoy over the past several years.

Taking the ramp onto I-74, he mused on his other problem—Eve. She was obviously none too pleased with him, since she seemed to think of him as an interloper, interfering with her family's business. He could understand that; after all, he'd warned Franklin that his daughter's reaction to losing out on the CEO position might be negative. Still, now that he'd reconciled that gorgeous, smoking-hot woman he'd shared the elevator with a few days ago with the snapping, angry-faced daughter of his mentor, he had another dilemma on his hands. How could he convince her to go out with him without further complicating an already awkward situation?

He was thinking so hard about it that the ride to his town house seemed to speed by faster than usual. Pulling into his garage, he entered his home through the kitchen door. No sooner than he'd stepped inside and closed the door, Chance bounded across the tile floor and jumped up to greet him. Giving the dog a good rubbing behind the ears, he smiled. "Missed me, boy? I've only been gone a couple of hours."

In response, Chance lapped at his face.

Shaking his head, he continued patting his furry buddy until he was content enough to get down and dash off to his doggie bed.

A bit later, Darius sat down at his kitchen table with a bottle of Corona and his MacBook Air. Opening it up, he booted it and surfed the internet for a few moments before landing on the Google search page. Curiosity about his new coworker got the better of him, and he typed "Eve Franklin" into the search box and hit Enter.

He heard someone banging on the door while he waited for the search results to populate. "Who is it?" he called out, the standard response to a door knock, even though he knew who it was.

"The police!" Rashad shouted the reply from the other side of the door.

Shaking his head, Darius got up and crossed through the dining room and the living room to get to the front door. Swinging it open, he stepped aside to allow Rashad in. "Hey, doofus."

"Hey, yourself." Rashad trudged in, his face twisted up into a frown like he'd recently sat on a tack.

Darius felt his brow furrow. "What the hell is wrong

with you? You look like you got your dick caught in your zipper or something."

Rashad pursed his lips. "Don't even joke about that shit, man." He followed Darius to the kitchen.

"Want a beer?" Darius sat back down by his laptop, gesturing toward the fridge with his head.

Rashad nodded, flung open the door. "I could sure use one, but I've gotta be back at the courthouse in forty-five minutes." He grabbed a can of soda instead, and joined him at the table.

"Sorry. Forgot you're still on the clock." He took a swig from his bottle as he scrolled through the search results on his screen.

"You're searching somebody on Google? A woman?" Rashad peered at the screen from his seat next to Darius.

"Yeah, nosy."

"Hmph." Rashad popped the tab on his soda and took a long draw. "I'll grill you about that later. Right now, I got my own problems."

Darius clicked on a result from Grambling State University's website, identifying Eve as the valedictorian of the class of 2003. "What's up, fool?"

Rashad leaned back in his chair. "One of the employees in the records room is suing my office for some so-called grievances he has."

Darius looked up from the screen. "Oh, shit. I bet the mayor ain't too happy about that."

"You better believe it. She's on my ass about this like a pack of hungry monkeys on a banana tree." He ran a hand over his face, and tugged the ends of his locks, bound in the ponytail he was forced to wear at the courthouse. "If I can't bring this to a swift conclusion, I can kiss my job goodbye."

Darius shook his head slowly. Rashad could be very

silly when he was with the fellas, but he took his job as register of deeds seriously. He had always performed his duties with honor and professionalism. It made him genuinely sorry to hear about his friend's troubles at work. "I don't know what to say, man. But I hope things work out."

Rashad scratched his chin. "Me, too. I'm the first black man to be register of deeds for Mecklenburg County. If I fuck up, who knows how long it will be before we get another brother in this position?"

He could only shrug in response. He went back to the article on his screen. He continued to read the impressive details of Eve Franklin's academic career at Grambling State while Rashad drank his soda in sullen silence. She'd been a stellar student at GSU, and the article mentioned her going on to pursue an advanced degree. Everything he read about her confirmed the perception he'd gotten from watching her present the financial reports at the board meeting. Eve was intelligent, accomplished and most of all, capable. Again he wondered why Joe Franklin didn't trust his daughter to take over the CEO position. Something wasn't adding up, and he planned to get to the bottom of it all as soon as he could manage.

Rashad cleared his throat. "So, the chick you're snooping on, who is she?"

He rolled his eyes. "I'm just looking into the particulars on my new coworker."

"Really. So is this the lady from the elevator, the one with the…" He made a gesture with both hands, tracing the outline of an hourglass figure.

"Yes. Turns out she's Joe's daughter."

"Damn." Rashad's eyes widened. "The way you described her, it's gonna be mighty hard to concentrate on anything while you're working."

Darius nodded. "You're right about that. But she's determined to deny the attraction between us. Something about an antifraternization policy."

Rashad set his empty soda can on the table. "Dude, don't get mixed up in something that'll get you in trouble. You don't want to have to deal with lawyers and all that shit."

"You're right, I don't." Darius knew there was truth in his friend's words, and he definitely wanted to avoid getting into any sort of sticky legal situations.

Still, he couldn't just pretend that Eve didn't set his blood on fire. There had to be some way to work around the rules at FTI; some kind of loophole that would allow him to pursue her.

Because at this point, no matter how much she tried to deny her feelings, pursuing her was a foregone conclusion.

Chapter 5

Uncrossing her legs at the knee and recrossing them at the ankle, Eve shifted on the stiff cushion of the chair. Why doctors charged so much to see patients, and then forced them to wait in hard, uncomfortable chairs, she couldn't fathom. All she knew was that she wanted this to be over as soon as possible, so she could get out of there.

Her mother and father had gone back into the examination room to see the doctor a while ago. Eve felt as if she'd been sitting there for ages. But the time on the wall clock across from her told her it had only been about an hour and a half. There was only one other person sitting in the waiting room. The old lady sitting several seats over had fallen asleep, her white-haired head resting on the wall behind her as she quietly snored. Beyond her, a wall of frosted glass windows revealed the shadows of people walking up and down the hospital concourse outside the office.

Reaching over to the small glass-top table next to her, Eve picked up an issue of *People* magazine. She flipped through the pages for several moments before realizing she didn't give a crap about what so-called celebrities were up to, then tossed the magazine back on the table.

A chill snaked up her legs, and again she wished she'd worn pants. In her haste to get out of the house this morning and beat the traffic, she'd put on a soft yellow skirt suit.

Had she been thinking clearly, she would've remembered that she'd be accompanying her parents to Dr. Crump's office today, where the air-conditioning seemed perpetually set on Arctic, and dressed appropriately. Already worried about what the doctor would report on her dad's health, she shut her eyes and let her head drop back against the wall. Maybe she could catch a nap like her white-haired companion.

A few minutes later, she felt someone tapping her on the shoulder. Opening her eyes, she saw the scrub-clad receptionist smiling down at her. "Sorry to disturb you, Miss Franklin, but Dr. Crump would like to speak with you."

Getting to her feet, Eve smoothed her hand over her hair, grabbed her purse and followed the receptionist through the swinging door behind the desk. They traversed a long corridor, passing several closed doors and cheerily dressed nurses before they came to the exam room where her parents were. The receptionist directed her inside, then stepped back and closed the door, leaving Eve in the small room with her mother, father and the doctor.

Dr. Cecelia Crump, her father's cardiologist, extended her hand. "Eve. It's good to see you again, dear." Her porcelain face barely showed her fifty-plus years, but the streak of gray running through her dark brown hair gave some hint of her age.

"Good to see you too, Doctor." Eve shook the woman's hand before taking a seat in the empty chair next to her mother. Her father sat on the exam table, wearing his trousers and shoes, but with a check-patterned hospital gown in the place of his shirt.

Dr. Crump seated herself on a swiveling stool that sat between the exam table and two chairs. "We've run a full workup on Mr. Franklin today, to get an overall picture of his cardiac health." She scooted over to the desk in the corner of the room and moved the computer mouse, bringing some charts and figures to the screen. "Some of the tests had to be sent out, and we won't get results on those for a few days. But the one's I've seen results for, I can't say I'm all that pleased."

Joseph's mouth dropped into a frown. "Oh, boy."

Eve could feel her heart pounding in her chest. "How bad is it, Dr. Crump?"

The doctor scrolled through the facts and figures on the screen as she spoke. "Your father's cholesterol is up, his blood pressure is way up and his arteries are showing signs of some plaque buildup. All this adds up to an above-average stroke risk, if he doesn't slow down."

Eve was no cardiologist, but she didn't like the sound of any of this. The word *stroke* in particular gave her a bad feeling.

Louise shook her head slowly, her face lined with worry. "I've tried to get him to do a little less, Doctor, but he's so stubborn. What are we going to do with him?"

Joseph grunted. "I am in the room, you know."

Dr. Crump wagged a finger at him. "And it's good that you are, Joseph, because I want you to hear this. I'm putting you on a strict diet to get these cholesterol and blood pressure levels down. And beyond that, you are not going back to work tomorrow."

Joseph cocked his head. "How long will I be out of commission, Doc?"

Dr. Crump's expression was serious. "I'm afraid this means retirement, Joseph. I think it's time to focus on taking care of yourself for a change."

He pressed his hand to his temple. "This is rough, Doc. I've been putting my all into FTI for the past forty years, and I can't believe it's ending like this."

Dr. Crump stood from her stool, placed a hand on his

shoulder. "You had a good run, Joseph, and your accomplishments are to be respected. But now it's time to guard your health so you can enjoy the fruits of all that hard work, all right?"

Joseph nodded, a crestfallen look on his face. "I understand."

Louise dashed away a tear. "We knew this was coming, but I didn't think it would be this soon."

Eve drew a deep breath, trying to hold back the tears threatening to spill. So this was it—her dad was finally retiring. She'd always thought that when the time came, she'd step into his role and run the company, maintaining the same high standards he'd upheld all those years. Now, things were so different from the way she'd thought they'd be, and she didn't know how to handle it. She looked at her father's face, and could clearly see how upset he was. Giving up control of FTI was obviously not going to be easy for him. The company was his baby, his life's work. She wanted to comfort him, but with the bitterness she felt inside, she didn't know how much help she would be to him.

She stood. "Thank you so much, Dr. Crump. I appreciate your taking the time to explain all of this to us."

The doctor offered a solemn nod. "No problem. I'm going to write up a few prescriptions for him, and then you and Louise can take him home."

Eve nodded.

Louise looked just as worried as Eve felt.

"Honey, do me a favor, call Darius Winstead, please."

Eve's eyes widened at her mother's words. "What for?"

Louise jotted a phone number on a slip of paper, then handed it to her. "To let him know we need him to start on Monday, instead of in two weeks the way we planned."

She took the slip of paper her mother held out and nodded. Part of her wanted to ask why she had to be the one to make the call. But she knew better than to ask. Her mother had made a request of her, and she'd do what she was asked regardless of her personal feelings. She slipped from the room and made her way to the waiting area. Extracting her phone from her purse, she dialed the number her mother had given her, bracing herself for what she knew would likely be a difficult conversation.

His left hand gripping Miss Molly's neck, Darius's fingers meandered over the strings of the bass as he plucked out the bass line to "Take the A Train." The song was a popular request during the Gents' gigs at the Blue, and he often practiced it when his bass was newly tuned. They played it so often he didn't need the sheet music.

He was so lost in the music that it took a few moments for him to become aware of the vibration on his hip. Setting Miss Molly gently in her stand, he reached to his left to turn down the stereo, then slipped his phone out of his jeans' pocket. "Hello?"

"Darius?" The sultry voice on the other end caught his attention.

It was Eve. Though their conversation had been brief, he'd recognize the distinct, melodic drawl of her voice anywhere.

"This is Darius." He listened for her response, curious as to what she might want.

"Oh, hello. Are you busy?"

"No." He knew he could go back to plucking the bass later. "What can I do for you?"

"My mother asked me to give you a call. I hope this won't be an inconvenience for you, but my father's been ordered to stop working by his cardiologist. So my parents are asking that you start working at FTI much sooner than originally planned."

His eyebrow lifted. "Okay. How much sooner are we talking about?"

She drew an audible breath. "Can you come in on Monday?"

Yikes. He had a Gents gig coming up this week, and had planned to enjoy his last few days of retirement at his beach house on Emerald Isle. "It's a lot sooner than we talked about, but if I'm needed, I'll be there."

She made a sound, but he couldn't tell if she was relieved or annoyed. "Thank you, I'm sure my parents will appreciate it."

Inwardly, he groaned, but he knew he was doing the right thing. He'd still have his evenings and weekends to himself, so the job wouldn't interfere with band practice and gigs. And maybe, just maybe, Eve would be trained and ready to take over the job faster than anyone thought. "I have to say, Eve, I'm not sure why your father asked me to do this. But he was such a good mentor to me, I'm glad I can do something to return the favor."

She was silent for a few moments before she spoke again. "Didn't he tell you why he asked you to come in? He doesn't feel I'm ready for the job." She said the words as if they hurt her teeth on the way out.

"He told me that, yes, but I don't agree."

"What?" Her voice conveyed a measure of shock.

He stood from the stool where he often sat while practicing, crossing the room to sit in his favorite armchair. "I was there in that board meeting, and I listened to you delivering the financial reports. Not only are you beautiful, but you're obviously damn good at what you do. If you can run the finance department with that much poise, there's no doubt in my mind you can run the company the same way."

"I...uh...appreciate that. Really, I do." Her tone had softened considerably, and he imagined her blushing.

"Just calling it as I saw it." He wondered if she would fuss at him for calling her beautiful, but he'd been telling the truth. She was the most attractive woman he'd ever laid eyes on. "I meant everything I said."

"I'll accept the compliments, but you recall how I feel about fraternizing."

"Who said anything about that?"

"So, you're going to drop those silly ideas about a so-called attraction between us, and keep things strictly professional?"

He chuckled. She certainly played being immovable well, but he knew better. When an attraction was this strong, it was only a matter of time before something happened. "Sure. I'll keep it just as professional as you do."

"Good." She seemed satisfied with his answer. "Then I'll see you at the office on Monday. Have a good weekend." She disconnected the call.

Pocketing his cell phone again, he felt a broad grin spread across his face. Eve was so sure she could deny what was happening between them, she had no idea what she'd just agreed to.

He'd promised to match her behavior, and he would. While she was certain that things between them would be all business, he knew better. The attraction between them was obvious, mutual and powerful. He wasn't going to press her about it; truth was, there was no need. It was only a matter of time until she gave in, and when she did, he'd be waiting.

Darius bopped into his kitchen the next morning, plucking an imaginary bass, as the sounds of John Coltrane flowing from his stereo filled his condo. He was looking forward to his usual Saturday ritual: a basketball game, lunch at the Brash Bull and rehearsal with the Queen City

Gents. It would provide a much needed break from his new coworker, Eve Franklin. There was something between them, something powerful. Shaking his head, he decided to think about something else besides his curvy colleague.

After pouring a bowl of kibble for Chance, he stepped to the refrigerator. He gathered four eggs, some Colby cheese and ham, then slid to the stove to prepare himself an omelet. He added a handful of diced bell peppers and onions. The spicy aroma soon permeated the atmosphere. He hummed along to the music as his breakfast sizzled in the skillet, and when it had browned nicely, he flipped it onto a plate.

Seated on his sofa with his breakfast, he turned off the stereo with his universal remote, and switched on the thirty-seven-inch flat-panel television mounted on his wall. Just in time for *SportsCenter.* The program's familiar theme song filled the room. Chance, having finished his food, took his usual curled-up position on a dog bed next to Darius. After enjoying his late breakfast and his first dose of sports news, Darius rinsed his plate in the sink and headed for the door. Rubbing Chance behind the ear, he grabbed his gym bag and left his apartment. Headed down the street on foot, he walked toward the nearby neighborhood where his best friend, Rashad McRae, lived.

The Sentry Heights development contained a mixture of ranch-style homes, apartments and condominiums, and featured plenty of amenities. There was a clubhouse with a gym and pool, laundry and dry cleaners on-site and twenty-four-hour security. Darius had almost bought a home there himself, but had found the neighborhood populated by too many teenagers for his liking. Still, that didn't stop him and his bandmates from making use of the available facilities with Rashad's resident pass.

Arriving at the basketball court, he found his bandmates

already there. Rashad leaned against the chain-link fence, his fingers flying across the screen of his smartphone. Darius often watched people using their phones, and took a measure of pride in knowing his invention had helped to add convenience to their lives. Conversely, for every parent he saw ignoring a young child in favor of their phone, or every driver attempting to use the phone while they operated a vehicle, he felt a pang of guilt. Who knew his little OS would affect so many people in such a profound way?

Marco stood by the fence, his knee bent behind him, his right ankle in the palm of his right hand. Ken sat on the gleaming metal bench, a look of concentration on his face as he laced up his basketball shoes.

"Afternoon, Gents," Darius called as he approached the fenced-in court.

"Hey," Ken called out. "You're late."

Darius rolled his eyes. "Whatever. You waited, didn't you?" He strode over to the bench, dropping his duffel bag to the blacktop near it. "Don't worry, Rashad and I are still gonna spank you on the court today."

"That's pretty big talk coming from a bassist," Marco declared in his heavy Hispanic accent. "Put your dinero where your mouth is."

"What are you trying to say?" Darius asked.

"The bass is very simple to play. All you have to do is pluck." Marco mimicked the motion on an imaginary instrument. "Now the saxophone, that's an instrument that requires some skill and coordination. That's why the ladies love me." He wiggled his fingers. "I'm good with my hands."

Darius punched his friend in the shoulder.

Rashad joined them, a basketball in hand. "All right, boys, curb the trash talk. You know the drill. It's me and Darius versus Marco and Ken. Winners choose the songs for Wednesday night's set." He paused, holding the ball up over his head. Darius and the others took their places around him. Releasing the ball, he shouted, "Put up or shut up!"

"Gimme that!" Darius snatched the ball from midair and took off down the court for the basket. Rashad, Marco and Ken followed. He zigzagged, darting here and there. In his mind, he stayed two steps ahead of his bandmates. Just as Darius pushed up to make the shot, a hand knocked the ball away.

Ken raced in the opposite direction, dribbling furiously. As Rashad and Darius ran to block him, Ken propelled into the air and thrust the ball up. All eyes watched as the ball crashed into the backboard and dropped into the hoop.

"Swish." Ken's single-word declaration was his idea of trash talk.

Darius groaned. "Don't get cocky. We ain't gonna keep letting that happen."

But it did, because Marco and Ken sank basket after basket. Darius did his best to defend against the onslaught, as did Rashad, who acted as if he were playing in the All-Star game. Finally, with the score an abysmal sixteen to one against them, an exhausted Darius trudged off the court.

Plopping down on the bench, he mopped the sweat from his brow, chest and the back of his neck with the blue-and-green-striped towel stashed in his duffel. Rashad joined him on the bench, stripping off his damp sleeveless shirt.

"Hey, man, what happened out there?" Rashad asked. "As soon as you got the ball, you let Mr. Zen and the Latin Lover over there grab it from you." He gestured to the grinning Ken and likewise satisfied Marco. "Where's your defense, D?"

"I gotta admit, my mind wasn't on the game." Darius groaned aloud. "It's this woman."

"Oh, Lord." Rashad threw up his hand, as if scolding Darius for letting a mere woman interfere with basketball. "Is this the same one you were running the poor man's background check on?"

"Eve Franklin."

Rashad's mouth dropped into a frown. "Seriously? Didn't we already talk about this?"

"I know, but I can't just stop wanting her."

"So everything I said, about the lawyers and legal troubles, that just went right in the garbage, huh." Rashad removed the rubber band holding his long dreadlocks in a ponytail.

"No, I was listening." Darius shook his head. "But have you seen her?"

Rashad's expression brightened. "Oh, man, I heard she's gorgeous. Is she?"

Darius nodded, picturing her, but trying to imagine what she'd look like if she actually smiled at him, instead of brushing him off. "The day I stepped on that elevator car, before I knew who she was, I couldn't help noticing how fine she was. Ever since then, all I can think about is those hips of hers—she's shaped like a Coke bottle, man."

Rashad appeared impressed with his description.

"I just wish she'd stop trying to deny her feelings."

"You seem pretty sure the attraction is mutual. What's so great about you?" Rashad joked.

"Shut up." Darius stuffed the towel back into his duffel bag, "I'm not some dude with an ego like a cocky rapper. But I know when a woman wants me, and trust me, Eve wants me."

Marco and Ken joined them on the bench.

Ken sat back against the chain-link fence. "I never let women affect me in that way."

"That's because you can't get a date," Darius shot back. He figured nothing short of nuclear war could rile Ken the Zen.

"I assure you, I can get a date. As soon as I decide I want one. But she will not distract me from my life the way this woman is distracting you." As if to show just how little he cared, Ken yawned.

Rashad shook his head. "We'll see about that. The right woman can make any man crazy, even you, Ken."

Marco addressed Darius in a mocking tone. "Well, you'd better get your mind right before the next game. Otherwise, you'll suffer another crushing defeat at my hands."

Darius scowled at him, then dismissed what he'd said. His growling stomach demanded to be fed. "Let's change and get over to the Brash Bull. I'm ready for some wings."

"All right." Rashad fished in the pocket of his cotton shorts and pulled out his keys. "We can change at my house."

Chapter 6

Eve's eyes scanned the various offerings laid out on the buffet line in the FTI dining room. She'd received a call from her father, asking that he meet her there for lunch so they could have a talk. Knowing he probably wanted to smooth things over with her, in light of the rift between them since her parents crushed her dream of becoming CEO, she decided to give him a chance to explain his concerns. Warring emotions still filled her, but she'd known her father to be a reasonable man, so she would hear him out.

As was always the case on Mondays, the usual soup, salad and potato bar was set up for the firm's employees. Sidestepping down the line with her bright red plastic tray, Eve filled her plate with a sampling of salad greens, tomatoes, cucumbers and carrots, topping it all with vinaigrette dressing. At the next station, she added a small bowl of tomato soup and a few packages of buttery crackers. Satisfied, she proceeded through the checkout line. After she'd swiped her badge, Eve left the line, intent on seeking out a table.

As she walked toward an empty table with her tray, Joseph entered through the swinging glass doors. He still looked pale, but wore a big smile on his face. "Hi, honey. Where are we going to sit?"

She stopped midstep to answer him. Mirroring his smile, she gestured to where she was headed. "In the empty booth over by the window."

"Okay. I'll join you over there as soon as I get my food."

As she opened her mouth to ask if he needed help, Joseph strode away, entering the buffet line.

Shaking her head, Eve walked over to the booth and set her tray on the table's blue lacquered surface. Sliding onto the bench, she watched her father's progress through the line. He seemed to be moving at a much slower pace than usual.

"Are you okay, Dad? Do you need me to carry your tray?"

"I'm fine," Joseph answered quickly. "Just need to get a little food in my system."

She was beginning to dress her salad when the chiming of her cell phone grabbed her attention. Producing the phone from her handbag and looking at the screen, she read the text message from Lina.

Any action with Elevator Volleyball Guy?

Eve shook her head at her friend's nosiness. After all her complaining about her own lack of a love life, Lina was still meddling in other folks' business. Deciding not to dignify the message with a reply, Eve chuckled and tucked her phone away.

Joseph joined her at the table a few minutes later with his own tray. When he sat down across from her, she noted the items he'd chosen: a baked potato with salsa on top, and a green salad with light dressing, along with a bottle of water.

"You're really doing a good job of eating better, Dad. I'm proud of you."

He grinned. "It's not as if your mother has given me

much of a choice, but I appreciate that." He forked up a fluffy portion of potato. "I wanted to talk to you about this thing with Darius and the CEO job. Your mother would have joined us, but she's upstairs supervising the folks who are cleaning out my office."

"I thought so. What did you want to tell me?" Her eyes drifted down as she stirred her soup.

"I just wanted you to know that this will only be temporary. You are still the rightful heir to Franklin Technologies, and one day soon you will step into your destiny as CEO." He sipped from his water bottle.

She continued to eat, remaining silent.

For a while, they both enjoyed their food in silence, until he spoke again.

"I think you still have some things to learn when it comes to investor relations, and dealing with the board of directors. Those things may sound minor now, but the cooperation from those two groups is integral to the running of the company. Everything else will fall apart quickly without those factors in place."

She took in his words, and could see some degree of truth in them. Even though she currently served as chief financial officer, there seemed to be a breakdown in communication between her and the other members of the board. Beyond that, she had so little interaction with the shareholders, she couldn't even speak on the subject with any authority. While she knew the ins and outs of the company and the software business, she knew she lacked working experience in the areas her father had pointed out.

He swallowed a mouthful of food, then rested his forearms on the table. "Eve? You've gotten awfully quiet. Do you understand where I'm coming from, honey?"

"Yes, Dad. I do. And I'm sorry I let my emotions get the better of me."

"It's understandable. I'm sorry I didn't let you know sooner that I was concerned about your professional development. But that's all behind us now, so let's make the best of the situation, okay?"

"Deal." She reached across the table to grasp her father's hands. "I love you, Dad. And I want you to rest up and enjoy your retirement."

"I love you, too. Don't worry, your mother is going to see to it that I do just that." He looked down at his nearly empty salad plate and the hollowed out skin of his potato. "You won't tell your mother if I have a little dessert, will you?" He wore a conspiratorial expression.

A smile touched her lips. She knew the new diet must be hard on him, so she shook her head. "I'll keep your secret, but don't get too crazy."

He slid out of the booth and went back to the buffet line, heading toward the end where various cakes, pies and other sweets were displayed. She concentrated on finishing up her own food.

The clatter of dishes and commotion coming from the direction of the line grabbed her attention. Turning to ascertain the cause of all the fuss, she gasped.

Her father lay on the floor near the dessert bar.

She rushed to his side, dropping to her knees next to him. "Dad!"

He didn't respond.

Several dining employees came over, including one who hopped over the counter.

Someone shouted, "Oh, no, Mr. Franklin's fainted!"

"Dad!" Eve's mind raced, her breath caught in her throat.

The elder Franklin remained as silent and still as a fallen oak.

"Get a doctor," she shouted to the gathering crowd of onlookers. Her wildly thumping heart pounded in her ears like a kettledrum. The cold, hard floor hurt her knees, but she didn't care.

She cradled her father's head in her lap, wishing she could love him back to consciousness. Urgency rose within her with each passing second. She shouted, "Stop standing around. Someone go get help!"

She searched the crowd, and saw Mimi pushing through. Her young secretary's face filled with concern. Pulling her earbuds from her ears, she stooped near Eve's side.

"What can I do to help, Ms. Franklin?" Her soft tone and familiar voice helped to soothe Eve's frazzled nerves for the moment.

"Call an ambulance. And send someone to tell my mother that Dad fainted."

Mimi dialed on her cell phone, and instructed a female employee nearby to alert Louise. Eve stroked her father's brow with trembling hands, sending up a silent prayer that her father would be all right.

Time slowed for her as she cradled his head in her arms. When the paramedics came, she watched as they lifted him onto a gurney and wheeled him across the crowded dining hall. Large tears welled in her eyes. *I've never felt so powerless.* Like a ghost, she followed the response team, wanting to at least see him make it into the ambulance.

Louise appeared on their heels, and together they raced out into the sunshine. Already, news reporters had surrounded the waiting vehicle. As she and her mother jogged out of the building, people began shoving microphones and cameras at them from all directions. She balled her fists at her sides, and her brow furrowed until she couldn't see. The downtown location of FTI presented a few downfalls, one of which being it's proximity to news outlets like the *Charlotte Observer.* The wails of the ambulance's sirens must have drawn the reporters out of their offices in search of a scoop.

Boisterous questions filled the air. She held her weeping mother close while the paramedics placed her father inside the ambulance. As it disappeared down the street, the reporters' questions continued, over the wail of the sirens.

"Mrs. Franklin, what happened to your husband?" one man called.

Another demanded, "Is it true that Mr. Franklin suffered a heart attack?"

"How will this impact the release of any upcoming software products?"

Her mind raced as she looked around for an escape from the questions peppering her like bird shot. Suddenly, she felt an arm lock around her shoulders. Turning, she looked up into the concerned eyes of Darius Winstead.

"Enough!" Darius shouted into a nearby microphone. "Enough. Can't you see that Mr. Franklin's health is in danger?"

Stunned at his take-charge manner, she just stared in his direction.

He bellowed again. "Now, I want all of you off FTI property in two minutes, or I'll request the Charlotte Police Department to escort you off!"

Gathering their equipment, the crowd of reporters and photographers dispersed. A few grumbled complaints could be heard, but none of them hung around to express their grievances.

Her breathing heavy and uneven, she turned to completely face him. "Thank you."

He nodded, his eyes still somewhat hard. "Let's get you and your mother to the hospital, so you can check on Mr. Franklin."

Eve's gaze fell on her pale, vacant-looking mother. "I'm sorry, Mama."

She nodded. "It's not your fault, honey."

Irvin Lane, the security chief, approached. "Miss Franklin, they've taken Mr. Franklin to CMCU. I've asked someone to bring your car around." As soon as the words left his mouth, a driver pulled the SUV up to the curb.

"Thanks, Irvin." Eve nodded his way, then let Darius guide her weary mother into the passenger seat of the waiting vehicle.

She held his gaze for a moment, and saw something almost imperceptible—an unspoken acknowledgment that touched her in ways she couldn't explain.

Breaking the contact, she stood aside for the driver to get out, then stepped onto the running board and climbed into the driver seat. She released the parking brake and put the truck in gear.

Tapping on the hood, Darius stood on the curb, watching the vehicle pull away with intense eyes.

Once on the road, she hung a quick U-turn, speeding down Trade Street toward Carolinas Medical Center-University. Once they arrived, Eve parked the car near the entrance and climbed out. She extended a hand to help her mother out on the other side, and they dashed inside.

She approached the woman at the reception station. Typing at a quick pace on the computer, the nurse didn't look up.

Eve didn't wait to be noticed.

"Excuse me, I'm looking for my father, Joseph Franklin. He came in by ambulance a few minutes ago." She flashed the FTI identification badge attached to the lapel of her soft gray business suit.

The woman looked up from the computer screen, peering at Eve over the monitor. "Yes, ma'am." She gestured to the double doors to her left. "Go through those doors, make a right and follow the green line. He's in bed seven."

"Thank you." She strode toward the doors, her mother in tow. Pushing her way through the doors and following the bright green line painted on the white linoleum floor, she led her mother by the hand.

Her father, a picture of frailty, lay on the bed in the small room.

Oh, Dad.

I've never seen you like this before.

He looked as if he was attached to every machine the hospital had at its disposal. The various monitors around him displayed everything from his blood pressure to his heart rate. Her ears rang with the symphony of beeps and blips the equipment emitted.

She stepped aside and let her mother enter first. Louise flew to Joseph's right side.

"I'm here, baby. Can you hear me?" Louise's voice was soft as she lay a gentle touch on his cheek.

Observing in silence from the other side of the bed as her mother cooed to her father, a small smile lifted the corners of Eve's mouth. After over forty years of marriage, it was obvious their love remained true.

"Hi, you must be Mrs. Franklin." A deep voice filled the room.

They both turned toward the sound. A young, olive-skinned man in a white medical coat entered the room. Louise addressed him.

"Yes, I'm Joseph's wife, and this is our daughter, Eve."

He moved farther into the room. He clutched a metal clipboard, from which his eyes never strayed. "I'm Dr. Raines. I'm a resident on Dr. Crump's service. I have Mr. Franklin's chart here, and I've ordered a series of tests."

She searched his face. "Do you have any idea what's wrong with my father?"

He shook his head. "Not exactly, but it's likely related to the cardiovascular illness Dr. Crump has noted in his medical records."

"Oh, Lord." Louise's whispered words conveyed her worry.

Dr. Raines moved to the heart rate monitor, examining the data displayed there. "His heart rate is a little faster than we would like."

Joseph stirred in the bed. All eyes in the room fell on him.

"Daddy, are you awake?" She grasped her father's hand tightly.

"Yes, pumpkin," he murmured.

"Joseph," Louise called, "I'm here, too."

"My love."

She noticed the blush filling her mother's cheeks.

"Well," Joseph rasped, "Looks like it really is time to pass along the reins." His eyes met Eve's.

She realized today was Darius's first day and she hadn't thought about it until now. "I guess so, Daddy."

A slight smile spread over his aging face. "Remember, it's only temporary. I'm sure you'll be ready in no time."

She sighed. *Great. This will make resisting Darius even harder.* "Okay, Dad. I'll help him hold down the fort until then."

"Good."

His eyes closed slowly, and as sleep claimed Joseph, his grating snores rose from the bed.

Dr. Raines chuckled. "He's quite right. He's certainly not going back to work now. We need to nail down what brought him here. Until then, we'll be keeping him here for observation." He removed another metal clipboard from the rack at the bed's end and tucked it under his arms. "Well, have a good afternoon, ladies. I'll be in touch as soon as we know something."

The doctor exited.

She took a seat in the armchair near her father's bed. "Looks like we'll be here for a while, Mom."

The big-screen television was tuned to the evening news, but Darius was only half listening to it. Sitting on the couch with Chance curled up next to him, he stroked the dog's head and thought about Eve.

Today had been his first official day as CEO, and he'd spent a good deal of it in Joseph Franklin's office—his new office. He and Mrs. Franklin had been making sure the movers got Joseph's things out, and putting his things in place to his liking. After he'd seen Eve and her mother off to follow the ambulance to the hospital, he'd gone back to complete the rest of the formalities the day held. But his mind had been elsewhere. He'd come home around four, changed into his sweats and prepared a light dinner.

Now it was after six, and he couldn't stand it any longer. He wanted to know what had happened to Mr. Franklin. The talking heads were already speculating about his condition. Moreover, he wanted to see how Eve was handling such a hectic, stressful day.

Remembering that she'd called him to let him know to come in today, he pulled out his phone and scrolled through the numbers in his incoming call list. He touched the screen to call the number back.

After two rings, she answered. "Hello?" Her voice held weariness.

"Eve? It's Darius."

Now she sounded surprised. "Oh. Um… Hi. How did you get my cell phone number?"

"You called me last week, remember?"

"That's right. Well, is there something you need?"

That almost made him chuckle. After all she'd been through in the past several hours, she wanted to know what he needed. "I needed to make sure you were okay, and check in on Mr. Franklin."

She took a deep, shaky breath. "That's very kind of you. They aren't exactly sure yet what's wrong with Dad. It's definitely heart trouble, though."

He nodded, as if she could see him. "Hmm. Okay, I hope they figure it out, and I hope he recovers soon. But how are you doing, Eve?"

Silence.

"Eve?"

"I'm…fine. Thanks for asking."

"You're welcome, though I'm not sure I believe you." He waited for the pushback he knew was coming.

"Darius, I told you I prefer to keep things strictly professional between us."

"I remember what you said. I still want to make sure you're all right, Eve." He leaned back on the sofa's cushions, scratching his chin with his free hand. Why was she so guarded? Getting her to reveal her feelings was like wildcat drilling for oil—hard work, and a total crapshoot.

"Do I have to go back to calling you Mr. Winstead?" A playful edge crept into her voice.

He knew she was deflecting his efforts to ascertain her feelings, so he decided not to push the issue. "No, that won't be necessary. Just promise me something."

"What?"

"That if you need something, you'll call me."

"But, Darius, we have staff that can—"

"No buts. Promise me."

She released a dramatic sigh.

"Promise me, or I'll come to the hospital right now and bug you in person."

"All right, Darius. If it will end this inquisition, then fine, I promise."

Her acquiescence was a small victory, yet he felt quite satisfied with himself. "That's better. I guess I'll let you go now."

"I appreciate your concern, but yes, let's stop before this gets any more uncomfortable."

"I'm not uncomfortable at all, Eve."

She blew a raspberry in his ear. "Bye, Darius."

The call disconnected.

Tucking his phone into the pocket of his sweatpants, Darius shook his head. Looking at Chance, he rubbed the dog behind the ear. "Women."

As if he understood, Chance moved closer and placed his head in his master's lap.

Chapter 7

Driving the next morning, Eve did her best to focus on the road. The haunting, melodic voice of Norah Jones flowed from the speakers as she wondered what the day would hold. As a child, she'd often gone to work with her father, and he would let her sit in the big leather chair at the end of the boardroom table. In those days, it had only been a game for her, but today, it would be all too real. Even though she wasn't in charge of Franklin Technologies, she felt responsible. More than anything, she wanted to make her father proud. After everything he'd been through over the past week, he deserved that much.

She stepped out of her truck, filled with trepidation. As she strolled toward the building's front entrance, an eager-looking young woman stopped her and thrust a large microphone into her face. A jeans-clad cameraman followed, and the lens was trained on her.

"Good morning, Ms. Franklin. I'm Polly Peterson with *News 12*. Do you have anything to say to the viewers, regarding your father's condition or the interim CEO of the company?"

Geez, these reporters never give it a rest! Grimacing, she looked into the camera. "It is my hope that my father will make a full and speedy recovery, and I will assist in any way I can in running the company he built." She paused, looking into the anxious eyes of the reporter. "Second of all, I don't like being ambushed, so if you want to interview me, schedule a time with my secretary. That's all I have to say." Whirling on her stiletto heels, she strode into the building without a backward glance.

Once inside, she made a stop by the security kiosk in the lobby. One of the younger security guards was stationed there.

"Good morning, Ms. Franklin. So sorry to hear about Mr. Franklin. How is he?"

"He's resting for now, until the doctors can determine what's wrong with him." She leaned over the polished marble desk, and lowered her voice. "Could you please direct your staff to be on the lookout for reporters? If you find any, escort them off the premises."

"Sure. I'll see to it, Ms. Franklin."

"Thank you. I have enough on my mind this morning without dealing with a bunch of them lurking around the building. Have a good day, Kevin."

She entered the elevator a few moments later, punching the button for the sixth floor. Just as the doors started to close, the short, balding Phillip Gordon came running across the lobby. "Hold the elevator!"

She rolled her eyes as she depressed the door open button. The little man, with that perpetual sour look on his face, joined her. As the doors closed he turned to her, looking as if he'd spent the entire morning sucking lemons.

"I don't believe for a moment that Darius character is ready to be CEO, not even on a temporary basis," he groused, adjusting his awful paisley tie.

His hot, foul breath filled the tiny space, and her nose wrinkled. It smelled as if he'd consumed garlic and orange juice for breakfast. She hoped he'd finished insulting Darius, if only to contain his rancid breath inside his mouth. But he continued voicing his thoughts.

"Furthermore, I think I'm a much better candidate. I worked in this company when that young buck was still in grammar school." He currently served as chief operations officer, and his discontent at not being appointed to the top board position was written all over his face.

She looked at him as if he'd sprouted a second head. "I knew I shouldn't have held the door for you. Let me come down to your level." Squatting a bit so she could meet his eyes, she lit into him. "My father made the decision to put Darius in charge. And to be quite honest, I've never cared that much for you. So if you ever speak about him that way again, I will be more than prepared to fire you, Mr. Gordon."

His eyes grew so large she thought they might pop out of his head.

The elevator car stopped, and the doors opened to the sixth floor.

She extended her hand, offering that he exit first. She trilled with false brightness, "Age before beauty."

Red from the top of his bald head to the base of his chubby neck, he stomped down the hall like a spoiled child put in his place. Enjoying the sight of him so put out, she followed him into the boardroom with a broad smile on her face.

As she entered the room, some of the board members stood, Louise included. She turned around to see Darius entering the room on her heels. Custom demanded all of them stand when the CEO entered, but she knew some of them didn't cotton to the idea of him being in charge. Mimi, who occupied a corner desk, ready to take down the minutes on her laptop, stood along with the others.

Bracing herself for fireworks, Eve took her seat next to her mother, while Darius sat at the end of the table.

"Good morning, everyone," Darius began, "I'm sure you all know why I've called this board meeting."

The few people who stood for him sat when he did. "To lord it over us that you were miraculously appointed to the CEO position?" Phillip Gordon quipped with a nasty sneer on his face.

He cut his eyes at the portly man, then pounded his fist on the table. "Mr. Gordon, are you calling Mr. Franklin's illness a miracle? Would you care to be demoted?"

A hush fell over the room. Mr. Gordon looked very uncomfortable.

She found Darius's show of authority quite attractive. Not that she'd ever tell him that.

"Or would you rather be summarily dismissed from your position?" He looked at the faces seated around the table. "I realize that many of you see me as too young and inexperienced to run this company. But those opinions have no place here. I've treated you all with respect." He narrowed his eyes. "I won't tolerate having my authority questioned. Until Mr. or Mrs. Franklin asks me to step down, I am in charge here. Is that understood?"

A chorus of affirmative responses erupted from the group.

"And Ms. Franklin is on equal footing with me, so be aware of that, as well." Darius turned to Eve, and once again, her insides reacted to his scrutiny. "Go ahead, Eve. You can handle it from here."

Wow. If he keeps looking at me like that... She didn't want to speculate on what that might lead to, so she focused on the task at hand. "Good. Then let's get started." She opened the briefcase she'd brought in with her and pulled out a stack of papers. "Ms. Fallon, could you raise your hand, please?"

Gloria, seated near the other end of the table, lifted her hand.

"Everyone, this is Gloria Fallon. She is the director of the finance department, where she's worked for fifteen years. For the time being, she will be taking my place on the board as chief financial officer, so I can assist Mr. Winstead. Please make her feel welcome."

A brief burst of applause filled the room.

Standing next to Eve, Darius elbowed her gently. "Call me Darius."

Feeling the heat rising in her cheeks, she looked away. "Is there anything else we need to address?"

"How is your father?" Li Sing Cho, chief technology officer, asked.

"The doctor says he's suffering from a cardiovascular ailment, but they've yet to pinpoint it. For now, he's resting."

Li Sing nodded. "I hope he'll make a quick recovery."

"Thank you. I'll relay that to him." She replaced the plans for the upcoming software launch party into her briefcase and snapped it shut. "With that said, I hereby adjourn this meeting. Mimi will forward the minutes to your inboxes by tomorrow morning."

"You're pretty good at this board meeting thing. Bores me to tears," Darius whispered for her ears only.

She chuckled before she could stop herself. Glancing his way, she found his chocolate eyes intent on her. "It bores me, too, to be honest. But I've been watching Dad do it forever."

"Well, I'm impressed." He stood, gathered his papers and pens. "I'm going back to the office. See you later, Eve."

And he departed.

As the board members filtered out, Louise turned to her. "I'm glad Darius put that grouchy Phillip Gordon in his place. If I had any say, he would've been fired years ago for his bad attitude."

"You're right." Even though being around Darius drove her to distraction, she liked the way he'd handled the old blowhard. She kissed her mother on the cheek. "I'm headed back to my office. I'll see you later for lunch, okay?"

Louise nodded, and Eve stood, clutching her briefcase. Mimi rose, laptop in hand, and followed her out of the boardroom.

Eve reclined in her bubble-filled whirlpool bathtub as evening fell. The sultry sounds of Sade's greatest hits filtered into the spacious bathroom as she sipped from a cold goblet of sparkling white wine. Placing the glass back into the holder on her bath caddy, she closed her eyes, resting her head on the plush pillow behind her. Humming along to the soothing music, she began to bathe with her favorite lavender-scented soap.

She emerged a short while later, clean and refreshed. In her large walk-in closet, she chose a comfortable ankle-length emerald satin gown. Slipping into it and its matching robe, she crossed the plush carpet barefoot into her bedroom. Freeing the latch and pushing the handle, she opened the French doors leading to her balcony. Once outside, she sat down on the cushioned rattan love seat, prepared to enjoy the late-August breeze. Her perch presented a great view of her wildflower garden and gazebo on the back lawn. Beyond the high black iron security gate and the stand of stately pines surrounding the property, the skyline of the still-bustling Queen City sparkled above the whizzing lights of the traffic streaming down I-77.

Watching the stars overhead, she heard the trill of the

ringing phone. Since the housekeeper had gone home for the day, she knew no one else would answer it. Rising from the love seat, she padded back into the room and picked up the receiver near her bed.

"Hello?"

"Eve?"

She recognized his voice immediately. "Hi… Mr. Winstead."

"I thought I said call me Darius."

She rolled her eyes, blushed a little. *He's not going to quit, is he.* "Okay, Darius. How are you?"

"I'm good, and you?"

"I'm well, considering."

"Any word on his condition yet?"

"No."

Silence filled the line for a moment. Then, he said, "I've been thinking we should get to know one another, since we'll be working together."

She folded her arms over her chest, aware of where he was headed. "Oh, really?"

"Yes. It's the sensible thing to do."

She knew what was on his mind, and there wasn't anything sensible about it. She clicked her tongue. "So you say."

"I know we're not on the same page when it comes to pursuing our mutual attraction."

"I never said I was attracted to you."

"You didn't have to. It's in your eyes, and on your face."

She said in a warning tone, "Darius…"

"Come on, give a brother a break."

A sigh escaped her. Part of her felt as if she was fighting a losing battle, but she wasn't ready to admit defeat just yet. "I'll try, because you were so helpful with those reporters. But if you mess up…"

"I'll fess up." He chuckled. "I can't ignore how you make me feel."

She didn't respond, choosing to concentrate on the sound of his voice. Giving in to her curiosity, she asked, "What do you do when you're not at work annoying me?"

He chuckled, apparently not offended. "I'm part of a jazz quartet called the Queen City Gents. I play the bass."

Surprise raised her brows. "Really? I like the name. Where can I see the Gents in action?"

"We have a regular gig Wednesday nights at the Blue."

She thought for a moment. "Oh, yeah. Is that the place in Hearst Tower? One of the accountants raves about the food there, but I've never been."

"That's the place," he responded. "What about you? What do you do when you're not being a high-powered executive?"

His deep velvet voice caressed her eardrum. *If his touch is as silky as his voice...* Would he make her tremble with anticipation? She thought it better to concentrate on his words, so she pushed her fantasies aside for later.

"Hmm. I love to read, play checkers, spend time with my best friend and hit the spa. And, coincidentally, I love jazz and neo-soul." She hoped he'd get the hint and invite her to one of the Gents' shows. Darius aroused her curiosity, among other things.

"I'll get you tickets to a show soon. But first, I want to take you somewhere where we can talk more. I want to get to know the real Eve Franklin."

The invitation in his voice set her mind ablaze with memories of his kiss. *And I'd like to sample those luscious lips again...* "I, uh, where would you like to meet?"

"Could I pick you up?"

She hesitated, unsure she really wanted to go down this path with him. She thought about the way he made her feel.

As much as she hated to admit it, she knew she couldn't conquer those feelings without exploring them further and defining them. "To be honest, I've dated my fair share of yahoos lately, so I think I'd rather meet you somewhere this first time." She waited for his response.

"I understand. Do you like Chinese?"

How does he know that? "Love it."

"Then let's meet at Cherry Blossom. Do you know where it is?"

"Yes."

"Great." He seemed pleased. "Let's meet there Thursday night at eight. Will that work for you?"

"Sure." *I'm looking forward to it already.* Suddenly, an idea struck. "Wait. Would you mind if I brought along my best friend, Lina?" Cherry Blossom was Lina's favorite Chinese restaurant, and Eve knew having her best friend along would relieve some of the pressure she often felt during first dates.

"If that helps you feel more comfortable, I don't mind. Tell you what. I'll bring along my buddy Rashad. Who knows, maybe the two of them will hit it off."

"Sounds good. I'll let you know tomorrow if she can make it." She could already imagine Lina jumping up and down at the mere mention of the word *date*, on account of her self-professed drought. "Well, thanks for the invite. If all goes well, then I'll see you Thursday night."

"I'll be on my best behavior. I can't make any promises for Rashad, though," he said, with a low, rumbling laugh. "I'll let you go. Good night, Eve."

"You, too, Darius."

She placed the receiver back into the cradle and fell back on her pillows, grinning like a giddy schoolgirl. It then occurred to her that she didn't know how he'd gotten her home phone number. He likely culled it from the company directory of board members, she thought. Right now it didn't matter. His eagerness to get to know her had begun to crack the icy wall she'd tried to erect between them. Perhaps if she spent a little time with him, she could get the pesky yearning she felt for him out of her system.

Parking in the lot of Cherry Blossom, Eve swung open her car door.

The place looks pretty quiet for a Thursday night, she thought, stepping out onto the pavement. She glanced at her watch. *Ten minutes after eight.* She gave the parking lot a quick scan, and saw Lina's navy blue sedan parked nearby. The personalized plates reading TALDRNK made the vehicle easy to spot.

Smoothing the front of the light blue knee-length sheath she wore, she entered the restaurant and looked around, hoping to spot Darius or Lina. Darius must have made reservations after she'd agreed to meet him, because they were already at a table. In the back left corner of the room, Lina waved both her arms wildly above her head like an air traffic controller. Smiling, she strolled over to the table. Darius waited there, with a tall, dark, dreadlocked man she assumed to be Rashad.

"Hi, everybody. Sorry I'm late." She slid into the empty seat next to Darius.

The man with the long locks extended his hand. "You must be Eve. I'm Rashad McRae. Nice to meet you."

"Likewise." She shook Rashad's hand, then turned to Lina. "Have you been on your best behavior?"

Lina scoffed. "Sure I have. Ask Rashad. He loves me already."

The look in Rashad's eyes held a mixture of humor and frustration. She hoped he'd packed his patience for the night ahead. *I love Lina like a sister, but my girl is a lot to handle.*

A petite waitress approached the table, handing out menus. "Welcome to Cherry Blossom. I'll be back in a few moments to take your order." With a polite nod, she walked away.

Perusing the menu, she could feel Darius's eyes grazing over her body like a caress. Looking up, she found him watching her. His gaze sent a shiver down her spine.

"If you keep looking at me like that, you're going to set my clothes on fire," she whispered.

"I can't help it. You are incredibly beautiful. But I'll try," he disclosed in that low, velvet voice of his.

His dark handsomeness and his charm were wreaking havoc on her. With him sitting so close, she inhaled the spicy, masculine scent of his cologne. She thought it best to turn her attention back to her menu, before his smoldering eyes led her down a path she wasn't ready to tread. Why she felt such an attraction to this man, who'd irritated her on sight, she couldn't begin to guess.

When the waitress returned, the group placed their orders. After she left with their menus, Lina spoke. "So, Rashad, what do you do? I feel like I've heard your name before."

"I'm the register of deeds for Mecklenburg County. What about you?"

Lina looked impressed. "I'm a lawyer at the Werner Law Firm. I've probably seen you around the courthouse before."

She watched her friend make small talk with Rashad, and noticed the uncharacteristic redness around the base of Lina's neck. Pleasantly surprised, she mused that Lina's "dating drought" might be coming to an end.

"Does she know about the band yet?" Darius asked as he sipped water from his glass.

"What band?" Lina's eyebrows went up.

"The Queen City Gents," she interjected. "It's a jazz quartet, remember? I told you about it."

"Oh, yeah. So what do you do in the band?" Lina asked Rashad.

Rashad answered easily, "Piano and vocals."

"You can sing?" Lina's eyes widened in surprise. Then she smiled. "Come on," she said, grabbing Rashad by the arm. "Let's get our own table. Eve, you're cool, right?"

"Sure, Lina."

She watched as Lina led Rashad away.

Lina called back, "If he tries to get fresh, just give a shout!"

As they walked away, Darius laughed out loud. "Is she always that—insistent?"

"You mean, pushy? Yes. She's been that way ever since college."

Amusement twinkled in his dark eyes. "Well, this is a fortunate turn of events. Now I don't have to share you."

A dizzying warmth flowed from him, touching her in places too intimate to think of in public. "Really? And what are you planning to do, while we're alone?"

He smiled, showing off two rows of beautiful white teeth. "Find out everything there is to know about you."

She fought the urge to trace his kissable lips with her fingertip. "That's going to take more than one night."

"I'm willing to hang in there for the duration. I'm sure my patience will be rewarded."

Her insides reeled from his declaration. But relief soon filled her when she saw the waitress approaching with their food. "You do realize this is just a one-time thing, to thank you for getting rid of those reporters the other day."

He winked. "We'll see about that."

Simultaneously annoyed and intrigued by his cockiness, she said, "You have to understand…we can't date while we work together."

"Why not?" Challenge filled his voice and his expression.

"Because it's not a good idea. Can we talk about something else?" Apparently the concept of fraternization was lost on the man.

The waitress inquired about the rest of the party. Without taking her eyes off Darius, she pointed in the direction of Lina and Rashad's new table.

As he forked up some of his chow mei fun, she noted the paper cuts on his long-boned fingers. She let her gaze travel up the muscled bulge of his arms beneath the pale yellow dress shirt he wore. When her eyes swung back to his face, his gaze awaited.

"Who's setting clothes on fire now?" he teased.

He caught me staring. Trying to hide her embarrassment, she picked up her chopsticks and captured a shrimp from her plate of lo mein.

"How did you learn to eat with chopsticks? I never figured it out."

Grateful for the change of subject, she answered, "I spent some time with my father in China, recruiting for our research and development department. We've found some bright kids here in the States, but a lot of them seem to lack the drive and the work ethic we want in our employees."

He looked impressed. "Where else have you been?"

"Hmm—Tokyo, London, Paris, most of the major cities. Some were business trips, because we want to expand into the European market. Others were vacations."

"Wow. You're pretty well traveled for someone under thirty."

She waved him off. "Under thirty? Are you pulling my leg?"

"Well, how old are you?"

"Usually, I would lecture you on how you're not supposed to ask a lady her age, but I guess I've given you enough grief already." She paused, smiling. "I'm thirty-four. How old are you, Darius?"

"I'm thirty-six. Born and raised in Tennessee."

"When did you move here?" She sipped from her glass of lemonade.

"After college. Rashad and I shared an apartment for a while, until he got the job downtown." He finished the last bite of his rice noodles. "What about you? Born in Charlotte?"

She nodded. "My parents came here in the sixties. Dad bought a struggling software company, turned it around, and you know the rest. I'm an only child, so someday, FTI's supposed to be mine..."

Her voice trailed off. Now that her father was in the hospital, she wondered if someday would come sooner than she'd expected.

"Eve? What's wrong?"

"I'm sorry," she said, brushing a lone tear from her cheek. "I'm okay."

"I know you're worried about your father," he said, extending a gentle finger to stroke her cheek. "You don't need to hide it from me."

"But we barely know each other, and we have to keep this professional—"

"I know. Still, I don't want you to feel uncomfortable being vulnerable around me," he countered. His finger traced its way to her chin, and he lifted her face to capture her gaze. "I'm not out to hurt you, Eve."

Exhaling slowly, she relaxed, letting him slip his arm around her shoulders.

"I'm still waiting to hear what's wrong with him," she said, her voice soft and trembling. "My mother's by his bedside most days. He's doing fine for now, but I just wonder—what does he have? How serious is it? It's driving me crazy."

He nodded his understanding. "I hope they can tell you something soon."

"If they don't, I don't know what I'm going to do. I can't take too much more of this." She sighed. "This was supposed to be a thank-you date, not a therapy session," she lamented.

"Hey, I'm just glad you feel comfortable enough with me to talk about these things. Like I said, I want to know you, warts and all."

She looked up into his smiling coffee eyes. "I don't have any warts."

"Well, how would I know that? They could be in places I haven't seen..." His voice trailed off as he swept his heated, appreciative gaze over her body.

She started to yell at him for being so fresh, but the sparkle in his eyes made her laugh instead. She gently punched him in the shoulder. Even the small impact with the solid mass of muscle hurt her fist. "Ow!"

He chuckled. "Stop abusing me." He stretched back in the chair, putting his arms behind his head. "You'll reveal those treasures to me when the time comes. I won't pressure you."

The very idea of slipping her clothes off in the presence of this man made her cheeks, and her core, fill with a familiar heat. *Treasures?* The way he'd referred to her body and all its parts made her feel decidedly special.

Then again, who knew? That could be a line he used on a regular basis.

Either way, nothing's going to come of it...we're co-workers. "Do you say that to all your girls?"

"I don't date very much," he replied, "and when I do, I much prefer women, like you, to girls. I haven't had a steady girlfriend..." He appeared thoughtful for a moment. "Since ninety-nine."

"What? You haven't dated since then?"

"I've taken a few ladies out for drinks, but nothing ever came of it." He turned the question on her. "I bet you're forever beating guys off with a stick."

"Not really. But I do seem to attract a wide variety of jerks and perverts."

"Oh, really?"

"Well, let's see. In the past six months, I've dated three guys. The first one was married and didn't think I needed to know. The second guy seemed a little too eager to marry and 'merge' our assets, and the third tried to get me to participate in a threesome on our first date. What do you think?"

"Wow. I think I'm lucky I coaxed you into coming here."

"You're damn right."

"Don't worry. Your crazy-guy streak is over. I'm sane as they come."

"That's good to know, but we're not going down that path, remember?"

"Hey, Eve!" Lina's voice broke into the conversation.

She turned around, and to her surprise, saw her friend standing over the table, holding hands with Rashad. "What's up?"

"The singer and I are cutting out of here. Will you be okay without me?"

"Yeah. I'll be fine." Eve waved to her.

"Later, *chica*." Lina turned to leave, with Rashad close behind her.

"Bye, Darius," he called. "It was nice meeting you, Eve."

And then the pair drifted out into the night.

Darius motioned for the check and paid it, while Eve tried to avoid his eyes. They were too intense, too inviting.

He rose from the table, gallantly extending his hand to her. "You ready to call it a night? Don't want to keep you out too late."

Nodding, she stood and took his hand, and he led her out into the muggy night air.

She unlocked the door of her car, and he grabbed the handle. As Darius opened the door, she stepped in.

"Good night, Eve. I'll give you a call."

"Good night, Darius."

After the door closed, she waved to Darius, standing on the sidewalk, bathed in the light flowing from the restaurant.

Where is this headed?

Chapter 8

Sitting on the balcony adjoining her bedroom, Eve sipped from a cup of coffee. She stared off into the distance at the sky, painted with the remnants of sunrise. She'd spent the night tossing and turning, her thoughts alternating between worries about her father and worries about the growing attraction she felt to Darius. Now, she'd given up, and come outside to enjoy the early-morning breeze, hoping it would help clear her head.

A beautiful day dawned over the Queen City, and the songs of cardinals and blue jays filled the air around her. A few yards away, the gardener trimmed the topiary display around her fountain. The bounty of every blessing she'd been given lay out before her, and she couldn't help thinking it was mostly due to her father's hard work. That sent a twinge of pain through her.

She put down the empty mug on the wrought-iron table and walked back into her bedroom. As she shuffled into her closet to pick out an outfit for the day, the shrill ringing of her cell phone jarred her. Retrieving it from her nightstand, she answered.

"Hello?"

"Eve. It's Mama. You need to get down to the hospital. They've figured out what's wrong with your father."

Eve's breath caught in her throat for a moment. *I wonder how serious it is?* "Okay. I'll be there soon."

Ending the call, she went back to the closet. Choosing a pair of dark denim jeans and a comfortable sunny-yellow blouse, she dressed quickly. Jamming her feet into ballet flats, she ran downstairs.

At the entrance of Carolinas Medical Center, Eve made her way to the door. After stopping at the desk to get her father's room number, she headed down the quiet corridor, following the green line painted on the shiny linoleum floor. The antiseptic smell of hospital disinfectant wafted past her nose. Taking an elevator to the fourth floor, she followed the red line until she came to the room where Louise waited at her father's bedside.

"Hi, Mom. I got here as fast as I could."

"Hi, baby. He's been asking for you," Louise said, gesturing to Joseph, who lay in the bed.

She eased across the room to her father. "Hi, Daddy," she whispered, looking into his heavy, but smiling eyes. "How do you feel?"

"I'm all right," he said, clearing his throat. "I'm just ready to get out of this bed, and out of this hospital before I go stir-crazy."

She chuckled, then turned to her mother. "So, where's the doctor?"

"He got a page," Louise replied. "He should be back in the next few minutes."

Nodding, she swung her eyes back to her father. "You gave us quite a scare, Daddy. From now on, I want you to take good care of yourself. And follow the doctor's orders. And—"

"I know, I know." Joseph groaned. "Don't make me listen to that again. I just got that same lecture this morning from your mother."

"Good morning, Miss Franklin." A deep male voice cut into their conversation.

All eyes turned toward the door, where a young, black man in a lab coat stood. He carried a clipboard, and a manila folder stuffed with all manner of paper.

"Good morning, Doctor..."

"Allow me to introduce myself. I'm Dr. Granger, and I'm on the cardiology team." He crossed the room and extended his hand to her and she shook it. "Dr. Crump is on vacation, so I took on your father's case a few days ago."

"Nice to meet you." She smiled. "So what can you tell us about Dad's condition?"

"Well, as I told your mother earlier, we're concerned that he might have suffered a stroke. Upon performing several tests, we've found evidence of what we call a transient ischemic attack, or TIA."

"What on earth is that?" Louise asked, her voice bursting with concern.

"It means that something temporarily cut off blood flow to a part of the brain. In Mr. Franklin's case, it was a small blood clot that's now dislodged itself."

"How did this happen?" She looked at her father, drifting back to sleep. "It seemed so sudden."

"Several risk factors can lead to TIA," Dr. Granger continued, "In this case, we blame atherosclerosis, or hardening of the arteries. Now, I know this all sounds very serious, and it is. From now on, Joseph is at higher risk for having an actual stroke. I'll prescribe him several medications and put him on a special diet to ease the stress on his body by reducing his cholesterol intake." He jotted notes on a piece of paper attached to his clipboard. "That being said, I'm going to allow you ladies to take him home. Do you have any questions for me?"

"How can we prevent him from having a stroke, or getting worse?"

"The medications will help, but aren't guaranteed to prevent a stroke," Dr. Granger explained. "A lot will depend on Joseph. If he is willing to rest, take his prescriptions and follow my orders, I think he will recover. It will take time, though. Anything else?"

Louise shook her head, never taking her eyes off her snoring husband. "No, thank you very much, Doctor."

With a smile and a wave, the young doctor departed, leaving the two women to watch over the man they both loved. Silence reigned in the room, broken by the sounds of the heart rate monitor attached to her father. She stroked his forehead before kissing it, then took her mother's hand.

"Mama, is there anything I can do?"

"No, baby. I'll take care of your father. I'll bring in a nurse to make sure he's doing what he's supposed to."

"Mama, I can take some time off. I can help you—"

Louise shook her head. "You know good and well where your father wants you to be. Behind the desk at FTI, helping Darius run things there."

"But, Mama..."

"Don't 'but Mama' me, Eve. That company is his baby. We bought it on the verge of bankruptcy, and he made it more successful than ever. There's no one else he trusts to take care of things. You've got to be there—I won't be able to get him to rest otherwise."

She acquiesced, releasing a heavy sigh. "All right, Mama. If you think that's best."

"I know it's best."

"I've got to get over to the office, then," she said. "I'll call you later to check on him, okay?"

Louise smiled. "I'll call you, if I need you. Focus on running that company. It's yours now, after all."

She's right. As his sole heir, when Joseph passed away, or became unable to run FTI, the company and all its holdings would be transferred to her. In a matter of days, she would be the real-life, full-fledged owner of a large software company with offices in Charlotte, London and Japan. The realization of all the responsibility that would come with the title rocked her. She kissed her mother on the cheek in parting and left the room.

Am I really ready to take this on?

Then there was the question of Darius. He would be running the company for the foreseeable future, so there was no way for her to avoid him—unless she could quickly get ready to take on the job herself. The members of the board would make that decision, so it was out of her hands. She pressed her fingertips to her temples, feeling a headache coming on. It was all too much to think about.

Darius sat behind Mr. Franklin's big mahogany desk, going through a stack of paperwork. So many things required his attention. Looking over the work that lay before him, he had to admit his role was a little more complex than he'd expected. Everyone needed his signature or approval on one thing or another. This "business" side of things had led to his burnout with the software industry. It would definitely take some getting used to, after spending the past several years in blissful retirement. He reclined the leather executive chair, stretched his arms behind his head.

At least the view's nice.

And not just the one of the city outside the window. Eve sat on the plush dark brown sofa across from him, poring over her own pile of papers. He'd asked her to come up earlier to help him navigate the minefield of office politics and attack his mounting workload. Since she now owned

FTI, she'd relinquished her duties as CFO. Her only job now was to keep him from screwing up.

She's all mine, so to speak. If only that applied outside the office.

He watched the graceful way her fingers plied the keys of her laptop, the pencil she held between her glossy lips and the loose wisp of her hair that she kept pushing out of her face. Her honey skin tone was accentuated by the light purple sleeveless dress she wore. The dress hugged her curves in all the right places. He especially enjoyed the slight swell of her cleavage visible above the neckline, where a tiny gold cross hung from a chain.

The woman was temptation personified. He needed her around, but she didn't make it easy to concentrate.

"Do you want to talk, Eve?"

She barely looked up from the computer. "About what?"

"About your father's wishes, what he'd want me to do. Since he's not coming back, I've got to get the information from you."

Still typing away, she said, "I know he wants this company run with integrity and transparency. The only other thing he wanted was to keep it in the family, but I ruined that for him, didn't I?"

The bitter tone of her last few words wasn't lost on him. "Eve, don't beat yourself up."

Tears she refused to shed stood sparkling in the corners of her eyes. "Don't start getting in my business, Darius. That's not included in your job description."

He shook his head. What a piece of work. Here he was trying to be sensitive and she was snapping at him again. "Excuse me, I just wanted to make sure you were okay."

She looked directly at him, her eyes filled with defiance. "I'm fine. I'm a grown woman, and I don't need babysitting."

Drawing in a breath, Darius went back to his desk. He thought he was getting somewhere with her, but she remained as guarded as when they'd first met.

She looked as furious as a plucked hen, as his grandmother Ma Beaulah used to say, but he had no idea why. Knowing further conversation would only frustrate him, he resigned to concentrate on the pile of work on his desk for now.

That didn't mean he was giving up, though. Beneath all that sass, there lay a vulnerable woman. He was determined to reveal her and redirect all her fire and passion in a manner they would both enjoy.

Chapter 9

Eve entered the FTI building, crossing the lobby toward the elevators. Stepping into the car, she started to hit the button for the eleventh floor. Finger in midair, she remembered… *Damn… I'm going to the twelfth floor.*

Shaking her head, she punched the correct button, then leaned against the car's back wall as the doors closed.

When they opened again on the twelfth floor, Darius stood a few feet away, talking to his secretary. He wore a coal-black suit with subtle dark gray pinstripes running through it. The suit, along with the light gray shirt beneath it, fit him well but still stretched across his broad, muscular shoulders. His beard was trimmed neatly, framing his full, soft lips. He looked so handsome, it made her eyes hurt and her nipples tighten beneath her blouse.

The man is made of sexy.

She stepped off the elevator car, head down, hoping to dash by him unnoticed.

As soon as she passed him, she heard him call, "Good morning, Eve."

Not wanting to be rude, she stopped, and turned to face him. "Good morning, Mr. Winstead."

"Hey, you're the owner. Technically, I work for you, so would you just call me Darius?" His easy smile brightened the room.

She nodded, and continued on toward the owner's office she now occupied. He followed her, his long legs easily matching her step for step.

"I know you said you want to keep this on a professional level," he drawled, so near she could feel his warm breath on the back of her neck. "But I'm not sure I can do that."

Staring straight ahead to avoid his chocolate eyes, she asked, "Why not?"

"Because I'm attracted to you, Eve."

That declaration stopped her midstride. She looked up into the dark eyes she'd been trying so hard to avoid. "Mr. Winstead… Darius. We've discussed this. We simply can't have a relationship."

He leaned against the corridor wall across from her. "You keep saying that, but I have yet to hear a good reason."

Inwardly, she groaned. She only hoped he would approach running the company with this level of tenacity. "Because I'm concerned about the future of this company—"

"And I'm not?" He folded his arms across his wide chest, and the suit stretched more to accommodate the motion. "If FTI goes under, I'll disappoint my mentor and good friend. So I'm going to do the best I can to keep that from happening. I don't know why you would assume otherwise."

His jaw was firm, his eyes hard. She'd insulted him, and even though it hadn't been her intention, maybe that was best.

She took the last few steps to her office and let herself in. "I'm not going to argue with you about this." She stepped inside, intending to close the door in his face, but he wedged his foot in the door frame.

"I'm not going to argue with you, either." He reached

out, and stroked his index finger along her jaw. "You'll come to me willingly."

She trembled at the fiery imprint of his touch. Her eyes slid closed for a moment, and she allowed the door to open.

He stepped into the room, and the woodsy scent of his cologne overcame her. She struggled to focus despite the heady aroma. She felt his large fingers wrap around her chin, and he began to tilt it up—

Regaining her sanity for a moment, she jerked away. "Have a good day, Mr. Winstead." Her tone was wintry, despite the heat of desire he'd set ablaze inside her.

His face twisted into a mask of confusion and frustration, but he didn't press her. Instead, he spun around and left the office.

Trembling, she closed the door behind him.

Darius stormed into his office, wanting more than anything to slam the doors. Refraining from such a childish reaction to rejection, he dropped down on the plush brown sofa and rubbed his throbbing temples.

He hated the way Eve kept rebuffing him. While he hadn't dated a lot, no woman ever crushed his ego this way. But what he hated most was that her argument was somewhat sound. Getting into a relationship with him could really complicate things at the company.

Having only been in his position for a short time, he had yet to finish reading the thick binder containing the company bylaws. Maybe there was a rule in there about fraternization between FTI employees. In all her protesting, she'd never specifically mentioned one, so he really didn't know for sure. But he supposed she had a right to be worried about how a relationship between them might affect the company in the long run.

Honestly, he had concerns about it himself. Mr. Franklin

put an enormous amount of faith in him by asking him to run the company. How could he betray that trust by doing something that could ruin FTI? He sighed.

If only she wasn't so damn gorgeous.

As crazy as it seemed, he couldn't help being attracted to her. On the day he'd met her, she'd been cold and dismissive. She'd come across like a real ice queen, and not someone he would want to spend a great deal of time around.

But that night at Cherry Blossom—he'd seen a different side of her. She was so matter-of-fact when she talked about traveling the world for business, but she looked so vulnerable when he brought up the subject of her father. A softness existed within her that he hadn't expected, and part of him wanted to seek it out right then.

Rising from the sofa, he made his way to his desk and booted up the computer. For now, work would be the distraction to keep him from going back down the hall to her office, demanding she talk to him.

He'd leave her alone, let her cool off—but he didn't know how long he could last.

Wading through an endless sea of email, Eve groaned. Her inbox overflowed with memos, requests and the occasional spam message. Answering the important ones and deleting the others would take a couple of hours. Still, she needed something to take her mind off Darius, so she plowed ahead.

Around eleven, she finished going through her email. Deciding that she might leave the task of screening emails to Mimi from now on, she rose from the chair and went into the section of her office she'd designated as a reading nook. There, on a short counter along the wall, sat a coffeemaker, a sink, tea bags, mugs and everything she could possibly need to make a snack. She reached into the small refrigerator underneath the counter for bottled water and a small container of fruit salad. Food in hand, she took a seat on the comfortable vanilla-colored sofa she'd brought in. She retrieved the book club selection she wanted to finish reading, Beverly Jenkins's latest, from the small table next to her and opened it to the place she'd last stopped.

Wrapped up in the suspenseful novel, she didn't notice Mimi until she called her name. She laid the book in her lap. "Yes, Mimi?"

"Do you want me to get you something for lunch, Ms. Franklin?"

Eve glanced at her watch. *It's already twelve thirty.* She'd lost all track of time when she'd picked up the book. "Sure. I'll write down my order for you."

After jotting on a legal pad, she tore the sheet off, and handed it to Mimi. As Mimi reached to open the doors, they suddenly swung open. Lina walked in, sidestepping to avoid a collision with her secretary.

"Hey, Mimi." Lina then approached Eve's desk. "Lunch in the office again? That just won't do."

Shaking her head, she turned to Mimi. "Cancel my lunch order. I'll go grab something with Lina."

"Yes, ma'am." Mimi pulled the doors closed as she exited.

"What are you doing here? And why didn't you call me to let me know you were coming?" Eve cut a false frown at her friend.

Lina rolled her eyes. "It was a spur of the moment thing. Come on, you know you need a break, anyway." She adjusted the pink-and-yellow floral-print headband that held back her Afro. Silver and gold bangles rattled on her wrist. "Let's go!"

"Where are we going, Lina?" Eve removed her purse

from her desk drawer, smoothed her gray pencil skirt, and stood.

"Let's go to Smokey Bones."

She looked down at her crisp white blouse. "Girl, I'm not about to come back here with sauce stains all over my clothes."

Lina grabbed her by the arm, pulling her toward the door. "Lighten up, Eve. You wanna stop on the way and pick up a bib?"

She burst out laughing. "You are a complete nut."

"And you are a stick-in-the-mud. Now come on. The bones are smokin'!"

Giggling and talking, she followed after Lina, leaving her office.

Chapter 10

Darius sat at the bar when Eve stepped into the Blue on Wednesday night, with Lina close behind her. As she paused to give her name to the door attendant, he let his eyes sweep over her lush beauty. She wore a dark blue cocktail dress, her full breasts accentuated by the low-cut neck, shimmering with silver sequins. The diamonds in her ears and around her delicate wrist sparkled beneath the overhead lights.

She caught his gaze, and waved to him. As she approached, he inhaled the intoxicating scent she wore. He extended his hand, and she took it.

"Eve. You look lovely this evening."

She gifted him with a small, but dazzling smile. "Thank you. You clean up pretty well yourself."

The black pinstripe suit with white shirt, red tie and matching fedora acted as standard stage wear of the band. "Thanks."

Lina, standing nearby, cleared her throat. "I believe you promised us a front-row seat?"

"This way, ladies." He escorted Eve by locked arms, and Lina followed them, to a table in the center of the main room, in front of the stage.

Once they were in their seats, he said, "I've got to go backstage. We always warm up a little before a set." He brought her sweet-scented hand to his lips and kissed it, reveling in the blush that filled her cheeks. "Until the show, my sweet." He then turned away from his beautiful guest and went to meet with the rest of the Gents.

Eve's face filled with heat as Darius walked away from the table. The gentle kiss he'd laid on her hand left her tingling in places very unrelated.

"Oooh," Lina cooed, giving her a gentle jab with her elbow. "Somebody's blushing."

She couldn't hide her smile. "He looks good enough to eat in that suit." And he did. She'd thought so from the first moment she'd seen him tonight. He was chipping away at her determination to keep her distance from him, and the experience was both frustrating and thrilling.

Lina agreed. "Who you tellin'? Girl, I can't wait to see Rashad in that getup." She snapped her fingers. "Mmm. Make you wanna slap your mama."

Drowning out Lina's silliness, she took a moment to absorb the atmosphere of the Blue Lounge. In front of the stage, couples and groups filled the low-lit room, sitting around the many white-clothed circular tables. The din of a hundred conversations, competing with the melodic sounds of saxophone music flowing from hidden speakers, filled her ears.

She inhaled the rich aroma of Mediterranean food being cooked in the kitchen. She could only see the swinging doors leading into the room, but she could identify the scents easily. The tartness of garlic mixed with the sweetness of basil and the savory scent of roasting meat. Everything added up to a classy, relaxed atmosphere. *A girl could get used to this.*

A burst of applause made her turn her attention to the stage. A distinguished-looking white man stood there, in front of an old antique radio-style microphone. He wore a dark suit and metallic tie that caught the spotlight.

"Good evening, ladies and gentlemen. Welcome once

again to the Queen City Gents' Wednesday Night Jazz Flight, here at the Blue."

A smattering of female cheers rose from the audience.

Lina's voice was a mixture of sarcasm and awe as she remarked, "They seem pretty popular."

The man on stage continued his introduction. "Tonight, for your listening pleasure, the Gents present a romantic set to get all you lovers in the mood. So please, welcome to the stage, Charlotte's finest jazz musicians, the Queen City Gents!"

The heavy blue velvet curtain slid open, revealing four well-dressed men in perfect formation. Their hats tipped to the front, pulled down over their brows.

A single spotlight hit the bass. Standing next to it, Darius raised his hat, stepping into the light. With sure fingers, he began to pluck a midtempo bass line.

Another single spot illuminated the drum set. Seated behind it, an Asian man lifted his hat above his brow. Raising his sticks, he began to tap out a rhythm on the kick tom and the high-hat symbol.

Next the light hit the saxophonist. As the Hispanic man, with his shiny dark hair touching his shoulders, raised his hat, the smooth sound of his sax joined the tune. *I know this song...*

The last spot landed on Rashad, behind the keyboard. He tossed his hat in one quick motion. It landed on the table in front of Lina. Smiling, he started to play the melody of the song.

Lina, eyes wide, started to say, "Are they playing—"

Before she could finish her sentence, Rashad's voice filled the room as he sang, "Turn off the lights..."

On cue, the house lights dimmed, and as the band continued to play, Eve's eyes locked with Darius's. He stared at her from his post behind the bass. *If I'm affecting his concentration, I can't tell.*

His fingers never missed a note. But his heated gaze threatened to straighten the curl out of her hair. Part of her wanted to flee, to run from his questing eyes like a frightened rabbit.

My God, he's sexy.

Try as she might, she couldn't tear her eyes away. He seemed to be having the same problem. The suggestive lyrics of Teddy P sung by Rashad didn't help matters. If Darius kept looking at her like a hungry lion eyeing a gazelle, she knew it would be a very long, eventful night.

The first song came to an end, and the band eased into a rendition of Luther Vandross's "There's Nothing Better Than Love," sans vocals. She looked down at the table, trying to avoid his gaze, but when she looked up, he still watched her. His eye drew her, coaxing her to let go of her fears and explore all that a relationship with him could be.

From the stage, Darius couldn't see much of the audience. But he could see the one person he cared to look at: Eve. He held her eyes in the dim light, and as he plucked away on the bass, he wondered if she could read his mind.

He knew he'd promised himself he'd stop pursuing her, but at this moment, with her in that low-cut dress, he didn't know how he'd keep his vow. Everything about her, from her glossy lips to the shyness he saw in her eyes, pushed him toward the limit of his self-control. He was compelled by an invisible but palpable force to make her his. Whatever he had to do, he would do it, until he finally broke through her stubborn resistance. Once she let him show her just how good it could be, he knew she wouldn't regret it.

She's a whole lot of woman.

When the set ended to thunderous applause, Darius took his bows with the band and then darted off the stage. Seated at the end of the bar, he ordered a shot of scotch from the barkeep. He drank it down in one long sip, and set the glass back on the counter.

Out of the corner of his eye, he saw Eve walking in his direction.

She hesitated, looked away from his face. Then she locked eyes with him.

He returned her gaze as she entered his personal space. The brown orbs glowed with what looked like desire, her cheeks rosy.

If he wasn't mistaken, she was embarrassed. The way her gaze fled from his, retreating to her shoes, almost amused him.

He stood, tilted her chin upward, and let his eyes tell her there was no need to be ashamed of what passed between them.

Neither of them uttered a sound.

He groaned low in his throat, wrapped his arms around her bare shoulders, savoring their softness.

She looked up at him, eyes filled with wonder.

He drew her face up again and brushed his lips against hers. She didn't dodge him, or protest. Instead, she melted into him.

Feeling her relax in his embrace spurred him to deepen this first taste of passion. As her arms wrapped around his neck, he opened her lush lips with the tip of his tongue, and drank deep.

She tensed.

What's wrong with her?

He broke the seal of their lips.

She darted away, quickly disappearing into the still dense crowd.

He scanned the room for her. Shoulders slumped, he dropped onto the bar stool.

She's gone.

Chapter 11

Swigging from his frosty mug of beer, Darius watched the Carolina/Wisconsin game on the big screen behind the bar. Around him, Ken, Marco and Rashad sat on the worn leather swivel stools at the Brash Bull, hollering at the television. All the other seats in front of the old gray marble bar were occupied as well, typical of Sundays during football season.

"Defense, man, defense!" Rashad shouted as Wisconsin stole the ball yet again.

"Ugh," Marco groaned. "I don't even want to see the rest of this game. Let's just get a table." He hopped down from his stool, beer in hand.

"It is pretty painful to watch," Darius admitted. He grabbed his beer and followed the others to their usual booth, near the pool tables in the rear of the restaurant.

"Can you believe that game? Carolina aren't even trying today." Rashad shook his head, settling into the booth.

"You know I don't care." Ken's words elicited groans from the others around the table.

"Yeah, we know, Mr. Zen," Marco said mockingly. "You just haven't realized the entertaining merits of professional football."

"Hey, guys." The waitress's voice cut into their conversation.

Her pert nipples stood like sentinels beneath the tight

Brash Bull T-shirt she wore. All eyes fell on her as she set down a plate of hot wings, accompanied by celery and carrots that would probably go uneaten. "Thought I'd refresh your wing supply."

"Thanks, Tiffany." Marco gave her a smile.

With a wink, she disappeared.

"They're not as hard-core as they like to think." Ken finished off his root beer. "Now, kendo, that's a sport that requires strength of mind, as well as body."

"Yeah, yeah." Darius waved him off. He had no desire to listen to Ken go on and on about Japanese martial arts. There were more pressing things on his mind. "Man, I'm going nuts."

"About what?" Rashad asked around a mouthful of a buffalo wing.

"About Eve."

"Her again? What's wrong now?" Marco wiped his fingers on a cloth napkin.

"We went out. Rashad was there."

"Yeah," Rashad added. "She brought along her friend Lina. She's a fiery little thing."

"Anyway," Darius continued, "she's ducking me. I know she's into me, but…"

Ken quipped, "She doesn't want to get involved because you work together, right?"

"Yes." He ran a hand over his close-cut hair. "I know she's right, but I can't shake it off. I want her. Why won't she give me a chance?"

"Who knows," Rashad said. "That's just how women are. One minute everything's good, the next they're screaming at you."

Ken agreed. "He's right. The man who figures out the fairer sex will be a rich man indeed."

Marco smiled. "I don't have any complaints about them.

Soft music, sweet words, and I win them over just like that." He snapped his fingers.

"It's the accent, lover boy." Darius punched him on the shoulder. "At least half the booty you get is because women think you sound like Antonio Banderas."

"Correction. Antonio Banderas sounds like me."

Rashad laughed. "Man, I don't know why your head hasn't exploded by now. It's so damn swollen."

"Will somebody tell me something? I can't think straight. She's under my skin." Darius was loath to reveal his agony to his friends, but maybe one of them could offer some insight.

"I can't help you, man. I'm not getting anywhere with Lina, either." Rashad polished off the last wing.

"What? After y'all got a separate table at the Cherry Blossom, I thought you'd hit it off."

"We did. But she's got some serious trust issues." Rashad rubbed his forehead, as if the thought of her gave him an immediate headache. "There is something big—I mean really big, going down at County, and I'm right in the thick of it. I can't tell her what it is, so she thinks I'm lying when I say I've got to take care of it."

Ken's eyebrow went up. "What's happening at County?"

"Fool, didn't you hear what I just said? It's big! I can't tell anybody until I get things straightened out." He threw his hands up. "The point is she automatically assumes I'm seeing somebody else."

"I expect you to let us know if you're in real trouble, man," Marco said.

"I know. And if it comes to that, I will. But right now, I gotta play it close to the vest."

Darius groaned. "Okay, so we've established that women are irrational, crazy and don't trust us. Now what? We pick up fake accents so we can woo them?"

Marco appeared insulted. Ken chuckled.

"Look, your guess is as good as mine," Rashad said. "But I'm in it to win it with Lina. Besides, I never back down from a challenge."

Ken spoke. "If she's already under your skin, you don't really have a choice but to try with her. After all, you lack my self-control."

"Shut up, Ken." He sent a chicken bone sailing.

Ken caught it in midair. "And my reflexes."

The others around the table groaned.

He shook his head. Ken had been right about the man who understood women gaining serious wealth. While he doubted that would ever happen, he didn't aspire to understanding the entire female population. He'd settle for understanding the one woman who was so good at arousing and infuriating him.

"So, Gents, I think it's about time we hit the road," Rashad said.

"Yeah. We've got to rehearse the set for this coming week. And since Ken and I won the basketball game—again—we've decided what we want to play."

"What?" Darius asked.

Ken replied, "A mixed set. Something more modern."

"A little Marvin Gaye, Teddy P and Barry White. That'll draw the ladies for sure." Marco looked very satisfied with himself.

"Whatever. Let's go." Rashad stood.

As they left the Bull, Darius's mind strayed once again to Eve. *She's like a puzzle, but I'm gonna keep collecting the pieces until I get the whole picture.*

Eve roamed into the conference room on the third floor Monday morning, briefcase in hand. She hoped she'd be able to focus on work, but she doubted it. The meeting today, with the managers of the research and development department, as well as Chief Technology Officer Li Sing Cho, pertained to a new software suite FTI planned to launch. As important as she knew this meeting would be, she already found it hard to concentrate. The kiss with Darius a few nights ago left her still simmering like an unattended teakettle. While she'd spent the past two days of the previous week dodging him, there was no way of avoiding him any longer.

Taking her seat at one end of the table, she accepted a cup of coffee from Mimi. Murmuring a thank-you, she found herself slipping away to Darius Land once again.

She could almost feel his warm, soft lips pressed against hers, his muscular arms wrapped around her waist…

"Ms. Franklin? Are you okay?"

"What?" Leaving her reverie, she saw Mimi standing nearby. "Yes. I'm fine. Why do you ask?"

Mimi replied, "Because you just put your pencil in your coffee."

Looking down at the bright yellow barrel and pink eraser sticking out of what used to be fresh coffee, she groaned. "Mimi, could you get me another cup?"

Mimi retrieved the cup and darted out, hiding her smile behind her hand.

Doing her best to pull it together, she looked around the table. Most of the board was already present and seated around the table…except Darius. She told herself she wasn't at all curious about his tardiness.

A few moments later, he strode in, looking gorgeous in his black suit and crisp white shirt with a cranberry tie. His briefcase in one hand, the other hand carried his sport coat, slung over his forearm. Taking his seat at the other end of the table, he shot her a wink. She could feel herself blushing, so she quickly looked away.

Darius began the meeting. "Ms. Cho, what do you have to present on the new accounting software product?"

"Mr. Winstead, we've prepared a presentation for you." Li Sing rose from her seat at the opposite end of the table. Two of the supervisors helped her set up a slide projector and white screen. Soon, as the lights dimmed, a logo appeared on the screen.

Mimi returned, setting a fresh cup of coffee in front of Eve. She took a sip of the dark, sweetened brew as she waited for the setup to end.

Li Sing launched into her speech. "We call this software MyBusiness Sapphire. It's a highly efficient follow-up to last year's MyBusiness Ruby."

Eve asked, "What makes the new software more efficient?"

"Well, Ms. Franklin, we've been able to add capabilities that weren't available at the time of the previous software's release. MyBusiness Sapphire will run on any operating system, including the less popular Linux system. Also, it features a fully functional mail merge system, compatible with all major word processors, that's specifically made to address invoices."

She nodded, impressed with the hard work the research and development team had obviously put into building the product.

Darius looked impressed, as well. "Have we decided on a price point for this product?"

One of the female R & D middle managers answered. "Based on the production costs for the beta version, we think we can offer it at a very competitive price, to rival that of Inuzaka's software," she responded.

Darius said, "Excellent. Did you bring a beta copy for me to test run?"

Li Sing handed him a disc in a paper sleeve. "Here it is.

We think we've gotten it running smoothly, for the most part." She then handed a second copy to Eve. "We thought you'd like one, too, Ms. Franklin."

Darius tucked the CD into his briefcase. "Give me about a week to check it out, and I'll let you know my thoughts. What does our launch timetable look like?"

Li Sing's thirtysomething male assistant spoke up. "We're hoping to launch by late October, early November. We want to get a jump on Inuzaka's next release, which is not due out until December."

Darius appeared satisfied. "Okay, sounds like a plan. Of course, Ms. Franklin will assist me in evaluating the software. Until I return my verdict on MyBusiness Sapphire, I'd like your department to work on new speech recognition software that accounts for regional accents and dialects."

Li Sing nodded. "Yes, Mr. Winstead. We'll start right away."

The dialect idea was good, and one Eve hadn't considered herself. Pleasantly surprised, she nodded her approval. Now she could see why his background could be an asset.

He rose from his seat and adjourned the meeting. When the board members and Mimi vacated the room, he folded his arms over his broad chest and watched her, waiting.

Clearing her throat, she asked, "Is there something I can do for you, Mr. Winstead?"

He looked annoyed. "Yes. First of all—" he slowed down, emphasizing each syllable "—call—me—Da-ri-us." He shook his head, as if he couldn't believe she hadn't gotten it yet. "Second, when are we going to talk about what happened?"

She shuffled papers, tried to look busy. "It was—a lapse in judgment on my part. I apologize."

He covered the distance between them so fast, there wasn't time to look away. His eyes burned into hers. "Eve.

It wasn't a mistake." He stroked her cheek with his index finger. "When are you going to give me a chance?"

She shivered. His masculinity overwhelmed her. He made her feel vulnerable in a way she never experienced. No matter how much it annoyed her, she had to admit her attraction to him wasn't going to go away. "Right now. I can't go on this way."

He smiled, toned down the intensity of his gaze. "I was beginning to think you'd never give in."

She allowed herself a small smile. "It still seems unwise, but I—I do want to see where this goes." She clasped his hand.

He nodded. "We'll go as slow as you want."

"We don't need to broadcast this, Darius."

"I understand."

He tilted her chin. She knew what was coming.

This isn't the place but… Lord help me, I want this.

So when his lips pressed against hers, she didn't protest. Instead, she let the kiss, and the arms of the handsome software phenom, sweep her away.

In time, he broke the contact. "I've got to get back to work."

"I know. I'm going to do the same."

He ran his finger over her lips. "I'll see you later."

He walked out, and she stood in the silent room for a few long moments, then followed.

As she pushed the up button on the elevator panel and waited for the car to arrive, she remembered Darius's heated gaze, his hot kiss. She'd felt like a teenage girl, hormones surging. If she didn't get a hold of herself, Darius would get just what his eyes were asking for. Smiling to herself, she stepped into the elevator and rode up to her office.

Seated at her desk, she picked up her desk phone. After

dialing her parent's number, she waited through three rings until her mother finally answered.

"Hello?"

"Hey, Mom. How are you doing?"

"Pretty good, considering," Louise replied.

"Considering what? Is Daddy giving you a hard time?"

"How did you know? Your father is not an easy patient." Louise yawned. "All day, he's complaining." She broke into her best impression of her husband. "I'm tired of sitting around here. I'm bored. I wanna go somewhere."

Knowing her parents' relationship, her mother was exaggerating, but not by much. "Come on, Mom. You know he's Mr. Do-It-All. He hates being restricted like this."

"I know. But I don't care what he says," Louise insisted, "I'm doing this for his benefit. And I refuse to lose him, so I'm going to make sure he does what the doctor ordered."

She didn't want to lose him, either, so she did her best to encourage her mother. "Well, good luck. Try to be patient with him. He's not angry with you, just his situation."

"I know, baby."

In the background, she could hear her father's muffled calls for her mother.

"I've got to go," Louise said. "Your daddy's calling me. I'll talk to you later."

"Love you, Mom."

"Love you, too."

She replaced the receiver, shaking her head. *Daddy can be so stubborn.*

Withdrawing the CD she'd gotten at the meeting from her briefcase, she took it out of its paper sleeve and slipped it into her computer's drive. After taking a pen and pad from her desk drawer, she clicked the icon on her screen and prepared to analyze the software. Memories of Darius floated through her mind. She could almost feel his muscular arms surrounding her, his hard, taut body pressing against hers…

"Ugh!" she groaned, trying her best to push the thoughts away.

The man was entirely too distracting.

Chapter 12

Flowers in hand, Darius got out of his car across the street from the FTI building. He hoped the fresh arrangement of yellow roses, violets, and lamb's ears would brighten Eve's day.

The workday had ended a couple of hours ago. When he'd left for the day, she'd remained in her office, insisting that she needed to catch up on some work. Knowing how pointless it would have been to argue with her, he'd left her alone. Now he was back, hoping to get their new relationship off to a good start. It had been a hard-fought battle, and he wanted her to see that when she'd finally given in, they'd both won.

As he approached the front door, she stepped out. As always, she looked beautiful. The stress she bore did nothing to detract from that. The short yellow dress and matching pumps she wore appealed to his eyes, as did her hairstyle. She'd left it unbound, and it fell around her shoulders like dark silk.

When she saw him approaching, her eyes lit up. He extended the bouquet to her, and for a moment, he felt like a hormone-crazed teenager professing his love for the class beauty. Shaking the notion, he smiled.

She took the flowers from his hand, looking pleased. "Thank you, Darius. They're lovely."

"I'm glad you like them. I thought you would."

She nodded, blushing. "You were right."

He extended his hand, she took it.

"Where are we going?"

He kept his answer short and simple. "For a walk."

She held his hand as she nuzzled against his shoulder. "Let me guess. That's all you're going to tell me, right?"

"Wow. Beauty and brains." He chuckled.

She didn't ask any more questions.

For a few minutes, they walked down Trade Street in silence. As he took in the sights and sounds of Charlotte—the tall buildings reaching toward the sky, the setting sun behind them and the first call of crickets—he realized that the woman clutching his hand outshone them all.

They came to a stop a few blocks from the FTI building, in front of the Charlotte Marriott. They stood in front of the gilded revolving doors at the entrance.

"What are we doing here?"

"I'm taking you to Cutter's." He ushered her inside.

"I've never heard of it." She followed him through the lobby, and into the lounge.

"Here it is." They entered, and he gestured to a nearby brown leather love seat.

She sat down, and he joined her.

"Do you want to talk about what happened today at work today?"

"No," she said, dropping her head onto his shoulder. "Do you come here a lot?"

"I come here to unwind." He traced a finger along her bare shoulder. "I had a pretty hard time concentrating today."

"This relationship is still pretty new." She smiled, covered her embarrassingly toothy grin with her hand.

Gently, he pulled her hand away. "Don't cover your mouth like that."

Dashing away a tear, she asked, "Why not?"

"Because it keeps me from doing this—"

He leaned in, tilting her chin, and pressed his lips to hers. She responded immediately, parting her lips. The feminine sigh he drew from her spurred him to bring her closer. Pressing her against his body and his heart, he deepened the kiss.

When he withdrew, she lay back on the cushion, looking breathless and dazed. "You've got to stop doing that."

"Why? You don't like it?" He knew she did, but part of him would enjoy hearing her admit that fact.

"It's not that—it's just that—"

"What?" He found her blushing cheeks so alluring, he kissed them both.

"I can't think when you do that."

"Good. That means I'm doing it right."

She gave him a playful smile. "You are a little too cocky, Mr. Winstead."

"And you, Ms. Franklin," he whispered, leaning in for another taste of her sweetness, "are entirely too gorgeous—"

His voice trailed off as his lips grazed the fragrant flesh of her neck, just above the top of her dress. He relished her sharp intake of breath as he placed a few scorching licks along her earlobe. She shivered.

Satisfied that he'd worked her up enough for the moment, he pulled away.

She looked up into his eyes and said, "I think you should take me back now."

He knew the look on her face. Passion was building inside her, and she wanted to run away like a doe fleeing a hunter. It pleased him to know he was affecting her, and that knowledge made him more willing to wait for her to surrender to him.

To that end, he stood and helped her up. "Then let's go."

They walked out of the lounge and left the hotel. In silence, they covered the distance to the FTI building. She looked so deep in thought that it made him curious about what was on her mind. He decided it was best not to ask her, not wanting to cause her any undue embarrassment. The lady walking beside him was the epitome of class and elegance, and he planned to treat her just as her status demanded.

"I'm parked over here." She gestured to her truck parked in the courtyard.

He nodded and escorted her to the vehicle. Helping her inside and closing her door, he continued, "If you want to talk, just give me a call."

In a velvet-soft voice, she replied, "Thanks."

"Drive safely."

She smiled. In a few moments time, he watched her taillights disappear down the street.

As he walked back to his own car, he smiled to himself. *What a woman.*

Eve sat at her desk, her eyes focused on her computer screen. She was so engrossed in doing a second run-through of the MyBusiness Sapphire beta software that she didn't see the light blinking on her desk telephone.

She was running the mail merge section of the program when Mimi's voice came over the intercom system. "Miss Franklin?"

Momentarily jarred as the interruption broke her concentration, she pressed the appropriate button on her desk. "Yes, Mimi?"

"Mr. Gordon has called an emergency board meeting. It will start in thirty minutes."

Why on earth would he do that? "Thank you, Mimi." As she turned off the intercom, she wondered what was going on. The company bylaws allowed any member of the board in good standing to call emergency meetings, with sufficient reason. But she had no clue what the reason in this case might be. But since Gordon was the chief operations officer, it could be any problem that fell under his jurisdiction.

She wondered if Darius knew about this.

With no way to know until the meeting actually started, she clicked the icon on the computer screen that would allow her to finish testing the software.

As the time of the meeting drew near, she left her office, with Mimi in tow in case notes needed to be taken. They boarded the elevator together and rode down to the sixth floor boardroom.

When she and Mimi entered, the young secretary sat at the small desk she usually occupied and began setting up her laptop.

Most of the members of the board were already present, Eve noted as she took her seat to the right of the head of the table. Across from her sat Phillip Gordon, an open binder on the table in front of him. Small beads of perspiration sat on top of his shiny balding head as he read the content of the binder's pages with rapt interest. He seemed completely unaware of her presence. She was about to call his name and ask him why he'd called a meeting when Darius strode into the room.

Her eyes met his, and he shrugged his shoulders. From his gesture, she assumed he had no more information about the reason for this meeting than she did.

He took his seat next to her and straightened his white

silk tie. Leaning in, he whispered, "So I guess you don't know what's going on, either."

She shook her head, and gestured to Gordon. "No. But I suppose we're about to find out together."

Darius sat up in his chair just as Phillip closed his binder and stood. With the binder closed, she could see that he'd been poring over the company bylaws manual.

Clearing his throat and clutching the lapels of his gray suit, Phillip began speaking. "Ladies and gentlemen, there's a good reason I called this emergency meeting, so I'll get right to it."

She was grateful for that, since his breath was just as bad as always. She seriously wondered if the man had seen a toothbrush since President Ford left office.

"Distinguished members of the board," Phillip continued, "it's time we update the antiquated bylaws under which this company operates."

She sighed. What was the old man getting at? Sure, the bylaws had been written at the company's founding in the seventies, and hadn't been updated since the nineties, but why in the world would he bring that up now? The company was already going through a transitional period…

Oh, boy.

Suddenly it occurred to her that Gordon might be asking for something specifically designed to make things hard for Darius, like imposing a minimum age for the CEO.

She glanced at Darius and found him watching her. She knew something was coming, something negative. In all the years she'd known Phillip Gordon, negative had always been his strong suit.

Before she could say anything, Darius changed his focus. Looking directly at Gordon, he asked, "What are you getting at? Do you really think now is a good time to overhaul the bylaws?"

Gordon's sneer was altogether unpleasant. "No, Mr. Winstead. I am only proposing one small addition to the bylaws at this time."

She searched her purse for a handkerchief, and, finding a lilac-embroidered one her mother had given her on her twenty-first birthday, she covered her nose with it. Gordon's breath was so bad, her eyes were beginning to water. When he was finished, she would present a motion of her own, one that forced the man to either keep his mouth shut or scope out some Scope!

Apparently Darius was losing patience with Gordon, as well. "What small change is that, Gordon? Why have you dragged us all away from our duties?" he demanded.

Gordon's smug smile spoke volumes. Calmly, he stated, "We need a bylaw that prohibits fraternization between board members and company employees."

Chapter 13

Darius felt the muscles in his neck and shoulders lock up like the lid on one of Ma Beaulah's mason jars. Had the pudgy, condescending Phillip Gordon said what he thought he heard him say? Through clenched teeth, he asked, "What did you say, Mr. Gordon?"

Looking thoroughly pleased, Phillip repeated himself, but this time with more command in his tone.

He had never liked Phillip Gordon, and now he knew why. The man was a parasite, the worst kind of self-serving, egotistical jerk he'd ever encountered. From the look on Gordon's face, it was obvious he thought his suggestion to be quite clever.

Darius did not agree. "And why would we need such a bylaw so badly you thought it was necessary to call an emergency meeting?"

Gordon gave him a strange, mocking look. "Why, Mr. Winstead. You of all people should know just why we need such a rule, and why it's so urgent." Then he gave a sidelong glance to Eve, whose expression was unreadable behind the handkerchief she clutched to the lower part of her face.

The boardroom filled with a murmur of whispers, and when he looked at Eve again, she looked as if she wanted nothing more than to hide beneath the table.

He, on the other hand, could barely contain the urge to flatten Gordon's chubby face with his fist. That was not the way a businessman carried himself, so, standing, Darius conducted himself in a businesslike manner. "Mr. Gordon, I'd like to thank you for your suggestion. And I'd also like you to take your seat."

Surprise filled Gordon's face, but he did as he was asked.

"Ladies and gentlemen of the board, is there anyone in this room who thinks Mr. Gordon's suggestion is pressing enough to be voted on right now, or even to have merited this meeting?" Darius stood, hands clasped behind his back, and waited. Silence reigned in the room for a few long moments. He glanced at Eve once again, and saw that she'd tucked the handkerchief away. A small smile touched the corner of her lips as no one answered or raised their hand.

Cutting Gordon with a hard look, he announced, "In that case, this board meeting is adjourned. Enjoy the rest of your day."

Without another word, he walked out into the hallway, with most of the board members streaming out behind. It was best he leave the room now, or he would be seduced by his baser urges and do the pudgy little man bodily harm.

The echoing of footsteps on the marble floor and the sound of several hushed conversations filled the space as he made his way to the elevator. As he passed the restrooms near the elevator, he heard the sound of someone clearing their throat. Figuring it might be Eve he turned around. Instead he found Phillip Gordon standing mere feet away, his fat fists propped on his wide hips.

Rolling his eyes, he asked, "Can I help you with something, Mr. Gordon?"

"Yes," he said, his face twisted into a frown, "you can

help me understand how I got passed over for a job that I'm more than qualified for. Especially by the likes of you."

Darius's hands balled into fists, and it took great effort to keep them at his sides. Maintaining the distance between them, he repeated, "The likes of me?"

"You know what I mean. Some so-called genius who couldn't hack it in the business, and who's more interested in plowing the boss's daughter than in running this company!"

Red, flaming-hot anger rose within him, and he closed the space between them in an instant. Aware of the security camera focused on him, he placed his arm around Gordon's flabby shoulders and turned them both so that their backs were to the camera. His outer demeanor remained professional, despite his irritation. Using a bit more pressure than the gesture required, he spoke quietly in Gordon's ear. "Listen carefully. This is the second time I've told you not to disrespect me, and it's your last warning. I trust you won't cause any further trouble for Miss Franklin or for me, because if you do, there will be consequences. Have I made myself clear?"

Gordon squealed, his head bobbing up and down in a quick, exaggerated nod.

"Good," he said, releasing him. "Now go do something useful, will you?"

Gordon scurried down the hall and through the door leading to the stairwell at a speed that surprised him. He had no idea the man could haul his girth at such a pace.

Satisfied that his point was made, he peered back into the conference room to see if Eve was still there. The room was empty, so he turned and took the elevator back up to his office.

Moving with ease through the quiet, almost empty Urbana Tea and Tonics, Darius carried the two teacups he'd just gotten from the counter. Sliding into the booth with Eve, he slid the green tea she'd ordered across the table to her.

"Here you go."

"Thanks." Her delicate fingers wrapped around the cup's handle, and she took a sip. A soft, purring sound escaped her throat. "It's very good."

"I told you. They only serve the best and freshest teas here," Darius commented, taking a long drink of his own herbal blend. "I'm glad you like it."

Her shy smile filled his heart. She set the cup down, looking into his eyes. "You know, I've been doing my best to figure out why you're so wonderful and caring."

He returned her gaze, knowing what she meant. "Waiting for the other shoe to drop, huh?"

"Well, yes. I haven't dated a sane, well-adjusted, non-jerk in a while."

He nodded. "I get that. I just want you to know that I'm not like the other guys you've been with." Reaching across the table, he took her hand. "I know it may take some time, though, because the best way to prove it—" he paused to kiss the soft skin of her palm "—is to show you."

The deep breath she drew as his lips grazed her skin betrayed her enjoyment. Unable to resist the lure of her femininity, he turned her hand and kissed its back. Then he treated her wrist to the same touch of his lips.

When he raised his eyes to hers, passion smoldered there. He drew away, not wanting to cause her embarrassment in public. She was a sensual woman beneath the businesslike demeanor she wore most of the time. From what she'd told him, she had reason to be wary of dating anyone, and even more reason to be cautious about dating him.

The attraction he held for the gorgeous, graceful, and powerful Ms. Franklin surpassed the physical. It was taking him into an unknown realm, a desire like nothing he'd ever felt before. It wasn't just about getting her in bed. He wanted, more than anything, to know her in the truest sense. He could imagine himself allaying her fears and sharing her triumphs.

The repercussions of all the emotions she elicited in him made him uneasy. When a man gave too much of himself to a woman, pain was sure to follow. So, he pushed his thoughts aside.

His teacup now empty, he asked, "Do you want to sit outside for a while? It's such a nice night." He wasn't ready to leave her. As of late, he wanted to spend as much time with her as he could.

"Sure." She drank the last of the tea in her cup, and stood. Taking his extended hand, she allowed him to lead her outside.

The crisp late-evening breeze played through her hair as they took a seat on one of the wicker sofas near Urbana's entrance.

The sun sat low in the sky, and the temperature had cooled quite a bit since the afternoon rush hour. The floral and fruity notes of the teas brewing inside the shop wafted out onto the night air. Faint notes of classical music being played on a piano nearby, the laughter and conversation of passersby and the occasional rumbling of the engine of a passing vehicle surrounded them. This was the Queen City on a typical late-summer evening. Alive with activity, yet peaceful enough to enjoy.

He placed his arm over the back of the seat, and she laid her head on his shoulder. She looked content, and that pleased him. He wanted her to feel comfortable with him.

He held her, enjoying the feel of her body close to his, when the bell on the door of Urbana chimed.

He looked up.

And saw his mother, Olivia, stepping out of the tea shop.

Maybe it isn't her.

As he stared at her, she stopped cold.

A look that combined surprise and guilt came over her familiar brown eyes.

It is her.

He said, with fake pleasantness, "Olivia. Long time, no see."

A confused Eve looked on.

Olivia propped her fists on her hips.

"Oh, so now you're calling your mama by her first name?" Olivia pursed her lips. "Show me some respect, Darius."

He jumped up, angered by her tone. "Respect? For what? You abandoned me and Pop just like yesterday's trash." He didn't like having old wounds opened in front of Eve, but since his selfish, sorry excuse for a mother insisted on being out in public, it couldn't be avoided.

Olivia groaned. "Oh, please. Get over yourself. I had to do what was right for me. Your dad understood that I belonged on the stage." She seemed to notice Eve for the first time, and cast a disdainful eye on her. "And who's this fancy flavor-of-the-week? Trying to get in her pockets or her panties?"

Eve's face fell. Before he could explain, she gathered her purse and stood. "I've got to go, Darius." She turned and walked the short distance to her car.

He called after her. "Eve, wait!"

She answered by slamming the door of her truck and starting the engine. Within seconds, she pulled away from the curb and drove off.

As her taillights disappeared down the street, Darius turned his rage-filled gaze on Olivia. She stood, arms folded, her face was filled with self-satisfaction.

It amazed him that, after all these years, she still thought of no one but herself.

"Is this how you plan to gain my respect?" he ground out. "By insulting my date? You're just as clueless as always."

Olivia's aging face creased into a frown. "Don't talk to me in that tone, Darius. I brought you into this world."

He towered over her. Only his father's echoing demand that he never, ever hit a woman kept him from knocking her down on the sidewalk. He stared down into her eyes, not trying to hide his contempt. "Yeah. Thanks for that. Now we're even."

He turned away from her and walked toward his car, clenching his fists.

"Darius, you come back here. Apologize to me!" she shouted in his wake.

But he didn't look back.

Chapter 14

The phone receiver held to her ear with her shoulder, Eve typed on her wireless keyboard as she listened to the voice on the other end. The chief marketing officer was going on and on about the packaging for the new MyBusiness Sapphire software. The man had been filling her ear with nonstop talking for the past twenty minutes.

Clicking the send button on the email she'd been typing, she finally broke in to his speech. "Yes, Mr. Kirk, I agree. Blue is a great color for the packaging. Why don't you run your suggestions by Mr. Winstead."

In a confused tone, he replied, "I already did. He said I should get final approval from you."

Stifling a groan, she placed her fingertips on her temple. "Was Mr. Winstead agreeable with your plan?"

"Yes."

"Then you have my approval, as well. Have a good day, Mr. Kirk." Before he could launch into another period of endless chatter, she dropped the receiver into the cradle, ending the call.

Using the intercom, she asked Mimi to summon Darius to her office.

He came a few minutes later, sticking his head inside the room through her partially opened door. "You wanted to see me?"

She nodded, and he entered, his masculinity overtaking the room in a way she hadn't expected. Impeccably dressed as usual, in a navy blue suit that looked tailored to his muscular, broad-shouldered frame, he smiled as he closed the distance between them. Just looking at him threatened to dissolve her focus and blow it away like magnolia blossoms in a hurricane.

He sat in one of the armless leather chairs in front of her desk, his intense eyes on her. "So, what can I do for you?"

Shaking off the effects of his übermasculine presence, she cleared her throat. "Did you tell marketing to get secondary approval from me on the new software packaging?"

He nodded. "I guess you have already spoken to them."

"Yes, I have." She blinked, trying to break the contact of their gazes. "Mr. Kirk yapped on and on for a half hour about the details before I could get a word in."

"Sorry about that. The man is pretty talkative." He leaned back in the chair, looking decidedly comfortable.

She reclined in her own chair, matching his gesture. He didn't need to know he made her tingle in places she couldn't discuss at work, so she played it cool. "Darius, if you're going to be CEO, you can't defer to me on minor issues like this. You have to be able to make these kinds of decisions on your own."

Apparently he didn't agree. "You're the owner. Your opinion is just as important as mine."

"Yes, on things that have a major effect on how we do business," she countered. "But software packaging? You don't need my approval on that kind of thing."

He looked as if he was thinking, then folded his arms over his chest. With a mock pout, he joked, "I guess I'll have to decide what to have for lunch all by myself."

She chuckled, thankful for the break in the tension between them.

"I don't want to screw this up. I owe your father a lot."

She nodded her understanding.

"But I don't just mean the running of this company." He stood, leaning over the polished wood desk. "I want things to work between us, too."

Hearing those words, she let her gaze drop. After what she'd witnessed between Darius and his mother, she couldn't help feeling unsure about having a relationship with him.

His eyes remained trained on her, his brow furrowing as if he sensed her hesitation. "What's the matter?"

She sighed. He was from Tennessee; didn't he know the old Southern saying about the way a man treated his mama? "I'm not going to pry into whatever is causing conflict between you and your mother, because it's not my business. But I left because I didn't want to be dragged into it."

His answering nod was slow and deliberate. "I'm sorry about that. I know Olivia was pretty determined to put you in the middle of it, the way she kept referring to you."

"You know, I was always taught that the way a man treats his mama is the way I can expect to be treated, so..."

He reached out, his fingertips grazing her jawline. "I've heard that before. I just wasn't thinking clearly. My relationship with my mother is contentious and almost nonexistent. But I would never mistreat you, Eve."

Looking up into his eyes and seeing the sincerity there, she believed him. Lord help her, she believed every word he said.

"I know." Led by the attraction for him that washed over her like a summer storm, she came around to where he stood. Perched on the desk's edge, she kissed him on the cheek. "I really want this thing to work."

"Then let's not end this, no matter what."

His husky voice, so close to the shell of her ear, the feel his warm breath made her tremble. "Darius—"

He didn't give her time to finish. He wove a hand into her hair, and his lips crashed into hers. He kissed her fully, deeply, until she felt she would melt into her pumps.

The sound of someone clearing their throat came from the other side of the room, caught her attention, and she pulled away.

Phillip Gordon stood in the open doorway, disapproval clouding his chubby face. "Well, what's this? The CEO and the owner fraternizing?"

She rolled her eyes. His condescending tone was not lost to her.

Darius's stern response cut through the thick tension hanging in the room. "Phillip, you just gave me the excuse I needed. You're fired."

He puffed up like a rooster, and shouted in Darius's direction. "Fine! I'm above working for you anyhow, boy! And you can bet this isn't the end!"

And he stormed out.

In his wake, she looked at Darius. She could clearly read the anger in his eyes, and she had to admit, Gordon's harsh words had upset her, too.

Not knowing what else to do, she leaned into his open arms and let him comfort her.

As Darius watched the audience from backstage at the Blue, he shook his head in amazement. Every week, the crowd seemed to get larger, and on this particular Wednesday the place was so packed the waitstaff could barely move around the tables to deliver food and drinks.

But of course the crowd wasn't his main concern. Eve was.

She sat at the table up front, the same table she'd been sitting at the first night he'd invited her. Things had changed a great deal since that first night, but he was glad she hadn't freaked out and run away once their relationship had been outed.

She looked so beautiful, and he couldn't drag his eyes away from her. She wore a hot little red sequined halter and a black pencil skirt. She crossed her honey-brown legs, showing off the sexy black heels she wore. He could easily imagine his hands gliding up and down the soft, silky skin.

Her hair fell loose around her shoulders, and large diamond studs glittered in her ears. She looked down at her cell phone, her fingers tapping the screen as if she was sending a text.

He knew she couldn't see him watching her, and he was glad. He hoped she would be listening very carefully to tonight's set, because he planned to woo her until she was powerless to resist.

"Darius!" Marco's harsh whisper broke through his thoughts.

He turned his gaze to Marco, standing there with his saxophone. "What?"

Marco rolled his eyes. "We gotta go on stage, that's what. Stop being a space cadet over there, and go get your bass!"

"Yeah, yeah. Hold your horses." He rose and opened the case he'd propped against the wall near him. Taking out Miss Molly, he smiled as he made his way onto the stage behind the closed curtain.

Ken perched on a stool behind the drum set, as expressionless as ever, and Rashad sat on the bench near the piano, arranging sheet music on the stand.

Rashad asked, "Hey, key of C, right?"

He nodded. "Yeah. You've got your delivery down, right?"

Rashad winked. "I always bring my A game to the Blue."

"Good." He set his bass on the wooden stand, and sat on his own stool. "This is a very important night."

Rashad winked. "I know. "Don't worry, we got it."

The guys grew silent as they listened to Bobby, the announcer, introduce them.

The heavy blue velvet curtain went up.

The spotlight fell on the band, and they launched into their own arrangement of Duke Ellington and Irvin Mills's "It Don't Mean a Thing (If It Ain't Got That Swing)."

As Darius plucked out the familiar, up-tempo bass line, he let his eyes settle on Eve. All around her, people rose from their seats, taking what little floor space they could find to dance to the catchy tune. She tapped her foot, but made no move to rise.

He could tell from the tight smile and the sway of her upper body that she wanted to dance, but didn't feel comfortable enough to let loose. Shaking his head, he wondered if she would ever emerge from behind her power-suit persona and have some fun.

As the set moved on into the rollicking rhythm of Billy Strayhorn's classic "Take the A Train," women began to crowd around the stage. Glancing over at his bandmates, Darius shook his head. Marco dropped to his knees, playing his sax before a section of his adoring fans, while Rashad ricocheted between playing the keyboard and extending his hand to a young woman up front. Rashad was the band's vocalist, and his playboy stage persona kept the ladies in the audience coming back for the show, week after week. Darius knew his friends could be hams at times, but he overlooked it. Whatever kept the fans happy was fine by him.

But tonight, all the women standing around the stage

blocked his view of Eve. He wished the crowd would disperse a bit, so he could catch a glimpse of his classy lady.

By the time they eased the tempo down for the last song in the set, a Gents original that he penned himself, the group around the stage had thinned out enough for him to see her again.

Locking eyes with her, he fingered the opening notes of the song. Rashad's voice rang clear, but quiet, in accompaniment.

Women in the audience looked pleased with the song, swaying from side to side.

The lilting harmony of the tune filled the club. He could see silhouettes of lovers embracing beneath the dimmed lights. He watched them for a moment before letting his eyes settle back on Eve. With each passing word and verse, he could see her expression changing. That gave him hope that she realized the song had been written for her.

As the song and the set came to an end, he and his bandmates took their bows, and applause filled the room. People then drifted to and fro, mingling, eating and enjoying themselves.

Eve approached the edge of the stage, a smile gracing her face.

He propped his bass against the wall. Covering the distance between them, he sat down on the end of the stage, near where she stood.

She touched his hand. "Fantastic show."

"I'm glad you enjoyed it." He inhaled the soft scent of her perfume.

"I thought that last song was especially moving." She looked into his eyes, waiting.

Looks as if she's on to me. "I wrote it. It was inspired by you." He reached out, tracing a gentle finger along her silken jaw.

She trembled beneath his touch. "I don't know what to say—it's beautiful."

He hopped down from the stage, never tearing his eyes from hers.

She came to him, and he enfolded her in his embrace. He lifted her chin, watched her eyes slide closed. Her glossy lips parted in sweet invitation. Leaning down, he pressed his lips to hers.

Her delicate fingers stroked the back of his neck as the kiss deepened.

He groaned, pulling her in as close as he could. He left her lips to explore the hollow of her neck, scented with the sweet, sensual notes of her perfume. His arousal grew, increasing to the point of pain. If he didn't have her tonight, he seriously thought he might explode.

He placed a parting kiss on her neck, then whispered in her ear. "Let's get out of here, or I'm going to make love to you on the stage—"

She gasped.

He waited for her response.

Finally, she nodded.

Taking her hand, he led her from the club through the side entrance, to the parking lot beside the building.

They reached his car first; she was parked two spots to the left of him. He opened his driver-side door, turned to her. "My place, or yours?"

She smiled, her eyes filled with a sexy amusement. "Mine. Follow me."

He watched the sexy sway of her hips as she strolled to her own car and got in. When she fired up the engine and pulled out of the space, he followed her. For the duration of the drive, he did his best to concentrate on the road, but thoughts of making love to her dominated.

Floodlights positioned on the front lawn illuminated

the mansion's beautiful hard-coated stucco exterior. He thought it a very nice place, although way too large for a woman living alone.

He pulled his car around the circular driveway and parked it near the front door.

He looked around as he got out, so aroused and hard that walking was difficult.

He went to her car, opening the driver-side door. Then he took her extended hand and helped her out. She led him up the eight steps to the door, and fishing out her key, popped it open.

"Nice house," he remarked.

"Thanks. I bought it as a thirtieth birthday gift to myself."

The sound of her voice seemed to make him even harder. *So much for distracting myself with small talk.*

"Come on in," she said, leading the way into the darkened foyer.

He followed her into a windowed room just off the main hall. The moon shone above the trees outside, casting a soft glow on the white furniture and carpet in the room.

Releasing his hand, she sat down on the sofa and patted the spot next to her. "Care to join me?"

She didn't have to ask twice. He sat next to her, and took her into his arms. The moonlight played off the sequins on her top, and desire shimmered in her eyes.

He pressed his lips to hers, drawing her closer as he leaned into the cushion, until she hiked up her skirt a few inches and straddled his lap.

He growled low in his throat, wanting to strip off her clothes and show her just how hot she made him. He wove his hands into her soft, sweet smelling hair, and kissed her even harder.

Without breaking the kiss, she began clawing at his

dress shirt, trying to undo the buttons. He shrugged out of his jacket and let her continue until she opened the shirt, baring his chest.

She slid down, leaving a trail of kisses over his cheek, neck and shoulder, until she lingered on his chest. Her searching fingers reached for the front of his pants, and as the silver clasp slipped free, he sighed.

She grasped the zipper pull—

And the shrill sound of her ringing cell phone filled the room.

"I'm busy." Her soft spoken words punctuated her tugging down his zipper.

The phone ceased ringing.

As he pulled her back up to his kiss, the landline phone began to ring.

She stopped cold. "Hold that thought. I've got to see what's going on."

He released the breath he'd been holding since she began undoing his pants, and lay back against the cushion. She went across the room to a side table, and picked up the extension there.

"Hello?" he heard her say. He could see her shapely silhouette against the sheer white curtains.

"Oh my God… I'm on my way."

Concerned, he asked, "What is it?"

She crossed the room and tugged his hands. In a tear-strained voice, she whispered, "It's Dad."

He stood, took a moment to zip his pants and buttoned up his shirt. "I'll take you wherever you need to go."

Keys in hand, he followed her out the way they'd come.

Chapter 15

Her breath coming in rapid gasps, Eve rushed into Carolinas Medical Center-University's ICU, with Darius close behind her. The antiseptic smell of the place filled her nostrils as she raced down the corridor. Her eyes darted around the waiting area, until she spotted her mother.

Louise sat in the corner near a wall-mounted television. She was leaning forward, her salt-and-pepper head resting in her hands.

"Mom!" Eve jogged to her side, crouching in front of her. "What happened? Where's Dad?"

Her mother looked up, her swollen, red-rimmed eyes locking with Eve's. "He's in the OR. The doctor says he had a massive stroke—" Fat teardrops spilled onto her cheeks.

Her mother's worry was as palpable as her own, but she wanted to be strong for her. She knelt on the floor, and took her mother into her arms. As she tried to soothe her, she gazed up at Darius, who looked on in sympathetic silence from his seat next to her.

His handsome face showed his concern. "Is there anything you need?"

She released her mother, rose to her feet. "Stay with her for a minute. I've got to find out what's going on with Dad."

He nodded, and she crossed the waiting room to the admissions desk.

"Excuse me, but could you tell me when Joseph Franklin will be out of surgery?"

The bespectacled nurse typed something into the computer, then said, "It will be about another two hours. They've just begun."

She stroked her now throbbing, sweat-dampened temples. This would be the longest two hours of her life. Having Darius there, however, offered her comfort. "Will someone be out to talk to us?"

The nurse nodded. "Yes, ma'am, just as soon as they can spare a set of hands. The surgery is very complex, and requires a team of medical professionals." The nurse reached out and patted Eve's hand. "I assure you, they will do everything they can for him."

It all sounded pretty serious. She offered the nurse a small smile in return for her sympathy, then trudged back over to the two seats occupied by her mother and Darius.

Louise had nodded off, her head resting on the back of her chair.

Knowing how her mother hated to sleep in public, she realized just how exhausted she must be.

Darius asked, "What did they say?"

She dropped into the empty seat beside him. "He's in surgery now. They'll send someone out to talk to us, but it sounds like it's going to be a while."

He looked thoughtful for a moment. "I see. What about you?"

She looked at him with questioning eyes.

"How are you holding up?"

"I'm fine." Her face said different, she was sure. *How can I tell him I'm more worried than I've ever been in my whole life?*

With a finger, he beckoned to her. "Come here. Sit with me for a minute."

Pensive, she leaned her upper body closer to him. Instead, he pulled her down onto his lap. Unable to fight him, she sank down and let him hold her tight.

It wasn't fair. Half an hour ago, the only thing on her mind had been making love to Darius until the sun rose. Now her father's life was in danger.

I wish I could go back.

Darius's deep voice broke through her thoughts. "Eve, it's okay for you to be worried about your father."

"I'm fine." She bit back the emotion.

He wrapped a gentle hand around her chin, and turned her to face him. His eyes burned into hers, searing away the facade she'd created. "No, you're not. You don't need to hide your emotions from me."

The kiss he placed on her lips was as sweet as a summer blackberry. "Darius—" A renegade tear slid down her cheek, and she looked away.

His voice was sympathetic, but firm. "It's all right, Eve. Stop trying to hold it in."

Inside, that stubborn part of herself railed against what she knew was coming. She needed to be strong. Falling apart simply wasn't an option.

Her father lay unconscious on a table right now, with a whole team of doctors operating on his brain. She was very aware that she could lose him in an instant. Even if the surgery went well, there was still a chance that the man she knew and loved would never be the same.

Her pulse raced, her breathing coming in short spurts. She could feel the cold, clammy sensation of her sweat-dampened palms as she clasped her hands together.

How can I live with that?

How can I go on without Dad?

A sob escaped from the prison inside her throat, and she dropped her head onto Darius's shoulder. At long last, she allowed herself to cry.

He rubbed her back, whispering in her ear, "It's okay. I'm here. I'll stay all night if you need me."

Her body shook, crushed by the weight of it all. Her world was falling apart, and she had no idea how to handle it.

Tears coursed down her cheek, splashing onto his shirt, but he didn't seem to mind. He just rocked and stroked her, whispering endearments until her crying and shaking subsided.

When she sat up again, she blushed. She knew she must be a mess of runny eyeliner and streaked mascara. He handed her a handkerchief from his pocket, and she wiped her face. Motioning to the dark stain she'd left on his shoulder, she said, "Sorry."

He shook his head, brushing it off. "It's fine. I'm sure my dry cleaner can get mascara out."

His smile salved her wounded soul. "Thank you."

"Hey, I'm here for you. You can cry on me anytime you need to."

She kissed his lips to show her appreciation

Then she heard her mother clear her throat.

She and Darius separated, and turned to face her.

Louise's face held many questions. "Is this what's been going on between you two?"

Darius looked guilty for a moment. "I'm sorry, ma'am. I know this makes things complicated for FTI, but—your daughter is very special to me."

"I understand." Louise looked wistful, as if recalling a long ago memory. "Love can be that way…you can't choose who you love."

She could feel the heat rushing to her cheeks. "Mom."

Darius coughed to cover his laugh.

Her mother covered a yawn. "I'm sure it's no surprise to him. Well, anyway, thank you for bringing my daughter here to see about her dad. I'm sure you have other matters to attend to."

Eve immediately recognized that her mother was testing him, and turned to Darius to see what he would say.

He shook his head. "No, ma'am. I'll be staying here, in case there's anything I can do for you or Eve. Anything I need to do can wait."

Louise nodded, her expression betraying that she was impressed with his response. "Thank you, Darius. I'm sure Joseph will want to talk to you when this is all over."

He smiled. "I look forward to it."

Eve watched their interaction, amazed. It was the first time her mother hadn't brashly declared her opposition to someone she was dating. She thought about the repercussions of that.

She sat back, in reflective silence, while Darius made small talk with her mother. Whatever question Mom threw out, he gave an answer, and a good one. Louise couldn't seem to rattle him, and Eve found that very attractive.

A brunette female doctor, clad in blue scrubs, complete with mask and hairnet, approached them. "Mrs. Franklin?"

"Yes, I'm Louise Franklin."

"I'm Dr. Tate. I've just stepped away from the OR to give you a status update." She sat in the chair next to Louise, and removed her face mask. "Your husband is in stable condition right now, but it's very touch and go. Right now there's no way to tell if we'll be able to repair all the damage caused by the stroke."

Tears welled in Eve's eyes again. "Is my father going to—" She couldn't bring herself to finish the question.

Dr. Tate replied in a soft voice. "We will do everything we can for him, but right now—we just don't know."

Louise brushed away a tear of her own, her voice shaking. "Thank you, Doctor Tate. Please keep us informed."

Dr. Tate replaced her mask and rose to her feet. "I will." And then she disappeared down the corridor.

He looks so pale, so still.

Eve sat by her father's bedside, holding his hand. Across from her sat her mother, holding his other hand. Behind Eve's back, the sun rose over the Queen City, but the dawning of a new day was shrouded by the darkness clouding her heart.

He'd come out of surgery about two hours ago. Though he'd survived, the next twenty-four hours would be critical for him.

As she looked down at the unmoving, drawn face of the man who'd raised her, she brushed away the tears that stained her cheeks. She wasn't even sure he knew they were there, gathered around his bed.

The shuffling sound of paper shoes on the linoleum floor caught her attention. Raising her gaze, she saw an exhausted looking Dr. Tate entering the room

Dr. Tate said, "Good morning, ladies. I'm at the end of my shift, and I wanted to look in on you and Mr. Franklin before I left."

Her mother smiled. "Thank you, Doctor. That's very considerate."

Dr. Tate nodded. "Mr. Franklin's not out of the woods yet. He's stable now, but by tonight, we should know more." She pulled the clipboard out of the holder at the foot of the bed, made a few marks. "He may suffer some loss of function. If he comes out of this, he will probably need a full-time nurse."

Full-time nurse? "What about his habits, his likes and dislikes? Is he still my dad?"

Dr. Tate's face looked grim as she shook her head. "Maybe. But with a possible loss of speech and motor skills—we'll have to wait and see."

Eve slumped down into her seat.

Dr. Tate waved, and left.

She sighed. Sitting here this way, knowing there wasn't anything she could do, made her feel restless. "Mom, I'm going to the waiting room. Darius is still there." She rose from her chair.

Her mother nodded, never tearing her eyes away from her dad's face. Stooping down to kiss her on the cheek, she made her way out of the room.

In the waiting room, she found Darius sitting in the same chair he'd been in earlier. He sipped from a paper cup, watching the news on the television.

As she approached him, he set the cup down on the small side table nearby. "Any news?" he asked.

She shook her head, flopping down into the chair next to Darius.

He took her into his strong arms, and she rested her head on his shoulder.

"I'm sorry you have to go through this, Eve," he said. "But I'll be here for you."

She looked into his dark chocolate eyes, and felt herself falling for him all over again. "What about you? Aren't you tired?"

"I'm staying." He kissed her on the cheek.

He. Is. Amazing. "Why are you doing this for me?"

He shrugged. "Why not? Don't you know you deserve to be treated this way?"

So she'd missed the memo. Since when did men start getting their act together?

An announcement over the PA system cut her enjoyment short.

"Attention in the ICU. Adult code blue, room 1123, main hospital. Repeat—adult code blue, room 1123, main hospital."

She sprang from her seat. "That's Dad's room! Oh my God!"

She took off at a run, and Darius followed her.

When she got down the corridor, the sounds of doctors shouting and the medical equipment being used filled her ears. Pushing her way past the scrub-clad medical staff to get into the room, she got as close to his bed as she could. She quickly glanced back and found Darius watching from the door.

Her mother's hysterical screams filled the room. "Joseph! Joseph! Don't leave me!"

A nurse grabbed her mother by the shoulders and pulled her away from the bed. "We need you to step away and calm down, Mrs. Franklin."

Her mother persisted. "That's my husband—take your hands off me! I've loved that man for over forty years—Joseph!" Her screams morphed and melted into sobbing.

As she peered over an unknown shoulder, she could see the medical team, trying to revive her father.

"Clear!"

The paddles pressed down on his chest.

A jolt of electricity raised his body off the bed.

Despite the charge, he remained still and pale.

She clamped her hand over her mouth. Panic shot through her like the voltage from the machine they used on her father.

"Daddy!" she yelled, hoping, praying he would hear her and wake up. "Daddy, it's me, Eve!" Large tears fell from her eyes.

He didn't respond.

Her mind reeled.

I can't bear to lose him.

Not now, not like this.

Not before she told him one more time how much she adored him, how much he meant to her.

One doctor, his brow damp with sweat, began performing CPR. As he counted off the chest compressions, she could feel her heart pounding.

After a few minutes, they tried the paddles again.

Her father remained as unmoving as a statue.

The doctor who had performed CPR shook his head. He wiped the sweat from his brow with the back of his hand, and eased away.

The other medical staff followed suit, backing away from the bed.

The heart monitor's monotonous tone filled her ears.

Oh my God.

He's gone.

A lone voice spoke. "Call it."

A monotonous response came. "Time of death, 07:32."

Her mother's anguished wailing faded.

The faces and lights in the bustling room slowed, then darkened.

Daddy. No. Don't die.

Please, don't die...

Strong arms surrounded her, supported her.

All became dark and silent.

Chapter 16

Darius stood by the window, looking out at the dreary Sunday afternoon. Gray clouds filled the sky, blocking the sunlight, as the heavy rain pelted the people rushing into the church from the parking lot.

He wondered where Eve was in that moment. He hadn't seen her since the day Joseph died. That had been Thursday morning, only three days ago, but it had seemed much longer. He'd watched her call out her father's name in that hospital room, saw the pain and helplessness in her eyes. He'd also seen how unstable she'd been on her feet, so when she started to sway and reel, he'd been there to catch her.

Turning away from the scene outside the church, he straightened his tie and flopped down in a chair. Around him sat Rashad, Marco and Ken.

They'd all come to the Mount Glory Baptist Church for Joseph Franklin's funeral. He wanted, more than anything, to offer something to comfort Eve and her mother, and he could think of nothing better than to pay tribute with their music. When he'd presented the idea to his bandmates, they'd agreed right away. Now, they sat in one of the church's Sunday school classrooms, waiting for the service to get under way.

He broke the somber silence. "Thanks for doing this for me, guys."

"No problem." Marco replaced the reed on his saxophone.

Rashad inclined his head. "We've got your back."

"So, have you seen her yet?" Ken asked.

Solemnly, he sighed. "No. I was there at the hospital with her, but I haven't seen her since then. She's taking time off work, of course. When I called her to let her know we wanted to play at the service, she thanked me, but—"

"But what?" Rashad leaned forward.

"She just didn't sound like herself. I just wish I could fix it, make her feel better somehow." He shrugged, searching for the words to convey what he felt. "I've only known her for a short time, but it hurts me to see her in pain."

"Uh-oh," Marco said, shaking his head.

"What?"

"Sounds like you're falling—"

Rashad cut Marco off. "Don't say it, man. You'll jinx him!"

Marco only smiled. "It's too late for that. Darius is in love."

A collective groan rose from Darius's three friends.

"What if I am?" He got up from his seat and went back to his post at the window. "You guys talk like it's a death sentence."

"No, man. Love is beautiful." Marco brushed his dark hair away from his face. "It just means you lose the thrill of the hunt and the joy of conquest."

Ken, stone-faced as usual, offered a shrug. "That's only if you're thrilled by the hunt to begin with. It never did much for me."

Rashad chuckled. "Shut up, Ken. Nothing gets a rise out of you."

One of the deacons poked his head into the room. "The choir is here, and we're ready to help you get set up."

Rashad stood. "All right, Gents, let's do this thing right."

Darius led the way, and they all followed the deacon down the short hallway, and up the stairs to the choir stand.

The somber but pleasant faces of the choir members, already seated, greeted them. Their dark blue and white robes bore the embroidered initials MGBC: Mount Glory Baptist Church.

He took his place next to his bass, propped against the piano. Rashad sat down in front of the instrument, testing the tune by striking a few keys.

Ken stepped down a level, to where a drum set waited. Next to him, Marco took his place on a stool, shifting his saxophone on its neck strap.

Darius looked out into the congregation. People filed in, filling the rows. A few early birds were already seated in the pews.

In front of the choir stand, an array of large floral arrangements placed in Joseph's honor filled the altar with color. Everything about the atmosphere in the church announced that Joseph Franklin had been well loved.

The field of flowers continued down both of the side aisles. Only the center aisle remained clear, so he watched the door there, sitting down on his stool.

Within the next few minutes, the large church filled almost to capacity, but the four rows up front were reserved for the family. Rashad played a selection of hymns as the mourners took their seats.

The somber-faced pallbearers rolled Joseph's dark blue, gold-trimmed casket down the center aisle and locked the wheels in place once they reached the altar. The funeral director opened the casket, and Darius regarded the well-dressed man lying in repose there. He wished he'd had more time to show his appreciation to the older man, who'd taken a chance on him by hiring him fresh out of college, and letting him into the ivory tower of the FTI empire.

So he vowed to play his music the very best he could, in the hopes that he could offer the family a measure of comfort. Music had been a salve to his spirit during his darkest days, and now he wanted to share a little of that with them, especially Eve. He couldn't imagine the pain she must be in.

Eve trembled on Irvin's arm as she eased away her father's casket. Irvin's steady presence, and that of her mother, offered her a small comfort.

With each step, she wondered how she would get through this. What would she do without her dad, the man who shaped her life?

She and her mother took their seats as the service began. The reverend preached a lovely eulogy for her father. But the greatest comfort she felt came courtesy of the Queen City Gents, who soothed her wounded soul with a beautiful rendition of her father's favorite hymn, "Just a Closer Walk with Thee." The lilting, soulful sound of the saxophone mixed beautifully with Rashad's piano music and his well-pitched tenor singing voice. The choir provided melodious backup for his solo.

When the last notes of the song faded, the church filled with thunderous applause and the rhythmic banging of tambourines as the choir began to shout, praising God for her father's life.

She drew in a deep breath, inhaling the jubilant atmosphere. *Now, this is how my daddy would want to be remembered.*

As the service ended, Eve, her mother and Irvin moved outside to the family limousine for the ride to the cemetery. The rain had stopped, the clouds began breaking up overhead and the sun peeked through. Irvin helped her mother into the car, then took his seat up front with the driver.

Just as she stepped into the car, a hand touched her shoulder.

She turned around and found herself face-to-face with

Darius. He looked incredibly handsome in his tailored dark suit.

"How are you holding up, Eve?" he asked, his voice and his face filled with concern.

"I'll miss him terribly, but I'll be fine." She reached out to gently touch his face. "Thank you so much for providing that lovely music. That was my father's favorite hymn, and he would have appreciated it."

Darius nodded. "Your mother told me. And don't mention it. I hope it offered you some comfort."

Her eyes burned into his. "It did. And so have you."

She sat down in the car, and he closed the door. She rolled the tinted window down. "I'll see you at the graveside?"

"I'll be there." He disappeared into the crowd of people spilling out of the church.

Later, at the graveside, she listened to the words the reverend spoke over her father's grave. She did her best to soothe her mother, but couldn't break through her inconsolable sorrow. With shaking hands, her mother placed a single white rose atop her father's casket, and Eve followed suit.

As she and Irvin walked her mother back to the car, Darius walked over.

Eve turned to Irvin. "Will you see her home, and look after her?"

Irvin nodded. "Of course, Ms. Franklin."

Eve turned her gaze to Darius. "Give me a ride home?"

He offered a small smile. "Of course."

Extending his hand to her, he guided her away from the grave and down the gravel drive toward his car.

Once inside, she buckled her seat belt, sighing. As they drove away, she cast sorrowful eyes on the black hearse parked by the curb.

She felt as if she were abandoning him, as absurd as it was. It just felt so wrong to be leaving him behind.

"He's always going to be with you, Eve." Darius's voice reminded her.

She turned his way. "Thanks. I needed to hear that."

They rode the rest of the way in silence.

When Darius pulled the car into the space in front of Eve's palatial home, he looked around. The last time he'd been there, darkness obscured some of the details. Seeing it now in the late-afternoon sunlight made it even more impressive. The manicured lawn stretched out in front of the house like a golf course, and a blooming wildflower garden adorned the east and west wings. The fountain centering the driveway depicted an angel, pouring water from an urn.

He got out, walking around to the other side of the car, and helped Eve out. She led the way up the steps, then unlocked the door. He followed her inside.

Again, they went to the glass-enclosed sunroom they'd been in Wednesday night. As they sat down on the white sofa, facing the windows, memories of her fiery kisses and her hands blazing the trail down his chest filled his mind. She'd been so hot, so ready, until...

He viewed her red, weary eyes with concern. She was hurting now, and what she needed more than anything was to be comforted. He could tamp down his physical desire for her, because he knew the time wasn't right.

She eased closer to him, resting her head on his shoulder. "I guess you remember the last time we were in here."

His eyes slid closed. "Yeah. But we don't have to talk about that now."

"Darius—"

He pressed a finger to her lips. "No pressure. I'm just here to comfort you, Eve." He paused, dragging the finger across her satin cheek. "I noticed you didn't cry very much at the church."

She stiffened. "Like I said, I'll be fine."

"I know you will. But right now, you need to stop putting on a brave face."

She sat up, pulling away from him. "Don't do this, Darius. My mother is hurting, and she needs me to be strong for her."

"Eve, she isn't the only one hurting." He used a firm, but gentle hand to turn her face to his, and gazed into her eyes. "How many times do I have to tell you? You're not made of stone. It's okay to feel."

Her lovely brown eyes filled with tears, and she sighed. "I—I can't. Come tomorrow, I've got to go back to my life."

He nodded. "You can. You're human."

She twisted in his grasp. "No—I'm a Franklin!"

"Eve, it's all right. No one ever has to know. I won't tell anyone you cried." He'd never known a woman so determined to deny her emotions.

An anguished sob escaped her throat. "Daddy—"

Her body shook with emotion, and she fell back into his waiting arms. Just as in the hospital, he soothed her with soft words and caresses. He let her cry, scream and shake until she'd released all the emotions she'd pent up so well.

She fell into an exhausted sleep on his chest, and he held her close. He remained still, because she needed to rest and he didn't want to wake her.

He watched her sleep, stroking her hair. The thought entered his mind that he could spend forever this way, touching her, holding her.

He groaned, letting his head drop onto the back of the sofa. Had Marco been right? Had he fallen in love with his beautiful coworker?

He thought about it so long that he tired himself.

As the sun descended from its post, painting the sky in shades of gold, violet and pink, he fell asleep, with Eve still in his arms.

Chapter 17

Eve sat on the couch in the owner's office. After a week at home, she'd returned to work. She'd grieved alone for the most part, allowing no one but Darius to check on her. Her mother, lost in her own grief, had spoken with her by phone but hadn't felt up to leaving her home.

Now, the time had come for her to face the reality of life without the mooring presence of her father. She wasn't sure if she could do it, but she had no choice but to try.

Around lunchtime, she watched the ticker tape go by on CNN when Lina stepped into the office, two large bags in hand. She wore her usual work attire, a white blouse and black pencil skirt and blazer. She'd flat ironed her bushy 'fro into a bob. A short gold box chain hung around her neck.

Sitting the bags down on the coffee table, she pulled Eve to stand. "Oh, sweetie, I'm so sorry."

Eve sank into her embrace, and they held each other tight. "I'm sorry, too. I shouldn't have shut you out."

Lina sat down, crossing her long legs, and gave her hand a squeeze. "It's okay. Everybody grieves differently. I'm just glad that I can be here for you now. I brought you lunch."

She sat down next to her friend, inhaling the heavenly aromas coming from the two paper bags. "Mmm. Smells like—ribs." She looked at the name imprinted on the bags.

"Eddie's Place! Oh, Lina, this is just what I need to take my mind off my troubles."

Lina smiled. "I know. That's why I got you the macaroni and cheese, collard greens and buttered rolls."

"I know you got the dessert, too, didn't you?" She fished around in one of the bags.

Lina reached into the other bag and pulled out a tin pie plate. "Would I go to Eddie's and forget the sweet potato pie? I got a whole one. Desperate times, you know."

She was so grateful, she could kiss her friend. "Girl, thank you so much."

"Don't mention it. Just pass me one of those sodas and a fork, I'm hungry."

She obliged Lina, and the two of them dug in to the delicious offerings.

After she'd eaten her fill, Eve groaned. "Oh, I can't eat another bite."

"Me, either. There's still half a pie and some ribs left," Lina said, stretching her arms above her head.

"Just stash it in the minifridge over there." She pointed at the wall. "I'll eat it one day when I need a snack."

Lina crossed the room, and placed the leftovers into the small black refrigerator Eve had gestured to. Returning, she sat down next to her again.

"What have you been doing this week, anyway? Since you haven't been taking my calls, I was worried about you." Lina's eyes locked with Eve's and waited.

"I've been home, reading, sleeping. I guess you could say I was hiding."

"So, you just shut the whole world out?"

"Well, everybody except Darius."

Lina's left eyebrow went up. "Say what?"

"Darius. He stopped by every day. Brought me flowers and wine. He'd eat dinner with me—hold me until I could get to sleep."

Lina's wide eyes, and her tone, conveyed astonishment. "Well, knock me over with a feather. When did you all become so close?"

"He was there Wednesday—the night Daddy had the stroke."

"Wednesday? I knew I should have gone with you to the show." A regretful expression crossed Lina's face for a moment. "There, as in at your house?"

Heat rose in her cheeks. "Yes. He wrote a song for me, and the band played it that night."

"Girl, I'm jealous."

"Anyway, things got—heavy, and he came home with me. We were on the verge of making love when the phone rang."

Lina wiped her brow, as if the story had made her sweat. "Well, did you ever pick up where you left off?" The last few words were laced with slyness.

She shook her head. "He's been such a gentleman. He really seems to care more about comforting me now."

Lina giggled. "You know, a man like that can offer his own special brand of comfort. And if I were you, I'd take it."

"Lina, you are such a freak."

"Hey, I'm just saying. If you've already started, it's only a matter of time."

"Oh, Lina, would you stop it?"

"You haven't told him you love him, have you?" Lina's knowing eyes held hers.

"No—I'm not sure I love him."

Lina waved her off. "Girl, please. I can see right through that shaky defense. If you were on the stand, you'd be going to the lockup, honey." She sipped from her can of soda. "I know you love him. He's the only person you let get within ten yards of you during the hardest time in your life."

Her girlfriend was on to something, she realized. But she didn't want to think about that, so she changed the subject. "What about you and Rashad? What's happening in that continuing saga?"

Lina smiled. "Stop trying to change the subject."

"Lina, I—well, maybe I love him. I don't know."

"You are lying to yourself, and you know it."

"I can't just come out and tell him."

"So you admit it," Lina said. "I think, if you give him a little time, you'll find out you don't have to say it first."

She stared at her best friend, noting the glint in her eyes. "What? You think he's in love with me?"

"I'd say there's a pretty good chance. Why else would a man go out of his way like he has for you, and not expect you to give up the panties?" Lina clapped her hands together, the way she always did when she pointed something out. "Yeah. Sounds to me like Darius loves you."

"If that's true, why hasn't he told me?" She folded her arms smugly across her chest, thinking she'd thrown Lina off the trail.

Lina wiped her hands on a napkin. "Please. He's a man. He'll tell you when he can't hold it in any longer, when it's unavoidable. You know that's how they operate."

No such luck. *If Darius confessed his love for me, would I even know what to say?* All this thinking about Darius, and where the relationship was headed, gave her a headache. "Isn't it about time for you to go back to work?"

"Oh, I get it. I point out the truth, and you send me away." Lina gave her a playful tap on the forehead, then glanced at her watch. "But it is time for me to go, or I'm going to be late. I don't want to hear my boss's mouth today."

They both stood, and Eve followed Lina to the office doors. "I'll give you a call later, Lina."

"You'd better. Especially when Darius professes his undying love for you." She batted her eyelashes, placing her hand over her heart in a dramatic gesture.

She laughed, embracing her friend. "Bye, Lina."

"Bye."

And she made her way through the big double doors, leaving Eve alone to think about all she'd said.

Eve stood by the windowed wall of her sunroom, a glass of Merlot in her hand. The setting sun outside created an inviting tableau of purple and gold that soothed her frazzled nerves with its beauty.

Darius stepped behind her, wrapped his strong arms around her waist. The warmth of his body enveloped her, and she leaned back into him, savoring the respite he provided.

He'd called her as she'd driven home, saying he'd meet her there. When she'd gotten out of the truck, he'd been waiting on the front steps, a welcome sight after the day she'd had.

Now, standing by the window, watching the fiery sunset with him, she felt at ease for the first time in what seemed like forever. The two weeks since her father had passed had gone by at a crawl, each day seeming longer than the day before.

"So, tell me how you're doing." He nuzzled her ear.

Smiling, she sipped from her wineglass and turned to face him. "Overwhelmed. I've got to get everything done for the MyBusiness Sapphire launch, and I'm swamped underneath a mountain of paperwork. The launch party is about a week away."

"I know that. I've already turned in my approval on

it." He looked into her eyes, probing. "I mean, how are you feeling?"

His emphasis on the last word struck her. She wasn't sure she wanted to get into talking emotions with him. "Better. I know I'm going to go the rest of my life missing my dad. But I think I'm over the initial sting."

"I'm glad to hear that." He gave her a quick peck on the cheek.

"I wish I could say the same for my mother. She's pretty much been locked in her room for the past sixteen days. I try calling, but her butler always answers. He assures me he's seeing to her needs, but I'm worried about her."

He nodded. "I can't imagine the kind of pain she must be feeling, after being with your father for so many years." He touched her cheek. "Let her grieve. I'm sure she'll come around."

She sincerely hoped he was right. She had no doubts the house staff would see to her needs. But if only she could take her mother's pain away, she'd feel much better herself.

He broke the silence. "I've seen the look my father has when he talks about my mother." He paused, as if not wanting to reveal too much. "And Olivia left of her own free will."

"I know it's painful for you to talk about her, so I appreciate your openness." Her fingertips traced the outline of his jaw.

He nodded, but said nothing else on the matter.

His manner let her know it was time to change the subject. She grabbed his hand, led him to the white sofa facing the windowed wall. "Let's sit down."

He followed her in silence, and they sat down on the plush fabric. She placed her wineglass on the table in front of them, and leaned back into the comfort and safety of his outstretched arms.

For a few quiet moments, they just sat there, listening to the sounds of the crickets' song outside.

"You should know that my father liked you a lot." She rested her head on his chest. "He had a lot of faith in you, and showed it by giving you the job."

He answered by kissing the top of her head and stroking her hair.

She lifted her eyes, looking into his. Desire burned there, as plain as a flashing neon sign. She brought her face level with his, dragged a finger along his lips.

He groaned low in his throat. "I don't want to be hurt like my father was." A flicker of pain crossed over his face.

She wondered where that had come from. "I'm not out to hurt you, Darius."

"I know." He ran a hand over his forehead. "But I still worry about telling you—"

She bolted up, scrutinizing his face. He looked conflicted, and she wondered what he was getting at. "What is it? You can tell me."

He closed his eyes tightly, reopened them. "I thought I could hold back, but I can't anymore—"

"For goodness sake, Darius, what—"

"I love you, damn it." He blurted the words out, then immediately looked away.

The tenderness in his words touched her soul. She turned him to face her, pulled him forward and kissed him with all the wonder she felt.

He stroked his tongue over her parted lips, dipping it inside. His passionate kiss drove her to new heights, and intensified her desire to share all with him.

She usually hated it when Lina was right, but this time might not be so bad.

Breathless, she pulled away.

He smiled at her in the waning light, eyes full of wicked delight. “Anything you’d like to say?”

She knew it hadn’t been easy for him to put himself out there, so she figured she owed him the same. She’d had plenty of time alone to reflect and consider her feelings. While she hadn’t wanted to admit it to Lina, she knew now that Darius had her heart, and there would be no going back. “It’s probably so obvious, you may as well know. I—love you, Darius.”

He kissed her again, a brief flicker of sweetness on her lips. Standing, he took her hand. “Let’s go upstairs.”

She looked up at him, eyes teasing. “Why?”

He helped her rise to her feet. “So I can make sweet love to you, baby.”

Confidence marked his tone. Her core tightened with the anticipation of what they would share. Shivering, she stepped forward, leading him into the foyer and up the staircase to her bedroom.

At the top of the stairs, her maid, Cora, dusted the console table. Seeing the two of them, she nodded to Eve, then made herself scarce.

On the heels of her quick departure, Eve pressed down on the gold lever, opening the door to her master suite.

Chapter 18

With searching eyes, Darius took in his first glance of Eve's bedroom. It had all the makings of a woman's boudoir. Lace curtains covered the French doors on one wall. The room was done in soft tones of blue, green and beige. The soft carpet gave way like cotton beneath his feet. Her king-sized bed centered the large suite. The gauzy green material draped over the canopy and down the sides, along with the plush comforter and about thirty different pillows, it looked like the bed of a pampered empress.

As she walked toward the bed ahead of him and sat on its edge to remove her pumps, he reveled in how good it felt to be invited into her most private place. He knew then that he would do everything in his power to make sure she didn't regret opening it to him.

Approaching her, he pulled his polo shirt over his head, along with the sleeveless T-shirt beneath. Tossing the shirt over the back of the fancy upholstered chair occupying the corner near the French doors, he stood before her.

With trembling hands, she stroked his chest, then his abdomen.

He knelt on the soft carpet, running his hands up her smooth, caramel legs. Beneath her white sundress, he stroked her supple thighs. When he looked up, he saw her untie the back of the halter neck garment. The front of the dress fell to her waist, revealing a pink lace strapless bra.

The sight of the lacy garment sent even more heated blood rushing to his manhood. He traced his index finger along the rounded fullness of her breasts. He moved to sit next to her on the bed, and she didn't protest as he reached around her to undo the bra's clasp. Once he freed the twin beauties, he treated himself to the dark nipples crowning them until she moaned his name.

His brain foggy with desire, he dragged the dress from her body. The sight of the matching lace thong she wore fueled the fire in his blood. Laying her back on the bed, he trailed slow kisses down the plane of her stomach, then lingered at her navel, dipping his tongue into the tiny whorl.

Eve could feel her thong being taken from her, but she didn't care. She shivered with desire, and at this point, he could do whatever he wanted with her, as long as the kissing and caressing didn't stop.

Apparently what he wanted to do was drive her insane…

She felt the first scalding lick against the pearl of her womanhood, and part of her sanity slipped away. He continued his erotic play, alternating between wicked licks and toe-curling sucks, and she parted her legs without a second thought.

His large hands rested on the insides of her trembling thighs, holding them apart. His mouth, hot and magical, gave her more pleasure than she'd ever known.

The sensations climbed until she raised her hips off the bed, her entire body shaking and shivering with the intensity of his skill. When she reached the epoch of passion, she came with a strangled cry that echoed through the otherwise silent house.

As she floated back toward the earth, she found him

watching her. His eyes glowed with a wicked satisfaction. Pulling him down, she guided his body on top of hers until the hard evidence of his passion pressed against her inner thigh. He stood long enough to slip out of his pants and into a condom, then rejoined her.

She raised her hips in soundless invitation, and a heartbeat later, he filled her. Having him inside her felt so wondrous, she began to climb the heights of pleasure again. The rhythm built, and she met him stroke for stroke until the sweet friction became too much. She moaned, loud and long, as her body pulsated with another powerful orgasm.

He continued a few moments more before he gripped her hips, growling his own release.

She held his sweaty, slick body close to hers, wanting to hold on to him this way for eternity.

Even as passion gave way to exhaustion, she knew that because of what they'd shared, he was now an undeniable part of her.

Darius stood in his bathroom mirror, brushing his hair. The sounds of Duke Ellington and his orchestra, on WJAZ's *Saturday Night Swing Party*, floated into the small, well-lit space from the stereo in the living room.

After applying a splash of cologne on his bare chest, Darius flipped off the light and made his way to the bedroom. He glanced at the digital clock on his nightstand. In about a half an hour, Eve would be there.

He'd invited her to come over and watch a movie with him, and get acquainted with Chance. He'd also come to a decision that would affect both of them, and he wanted to tell her about it in private. After pulling on the gray silk shirt he'd chosen, he fastened the column of buttons going down the front.

As he slid into the kitchen to put away the clean dishes

in the dish rack, he heard a whimper at his feet. He looked down into the big brown eyes of his golden retriever, who pawed at his sock-clad foot.

He chuckled. "Don't worry, buddy. I haven't forgotten about you." Opening the lower cabinet next to his refrigerator, he pulled out the bag of dog food he kept there. Pouring Chance a dish of it, and setting it down on the floor with a full dish of water to accompany it, he went into the living room. Once he'd shut off the radio he flopped down on the couch.

With the remote, he turned on the TV. It always stayed on ESPN, and he found himself right in the middle of the six-o'clock *SportsCenter* broadcast. The ticker tape whizzed by with the day's sports scores, and he scanned it for the results of his favorite matchups.

Just as the show came to an end, a knock sounded at the front door. As he always did, Chance bounded to the door, filling the room with loud barks.

"Chance, chill out." Darius crossed the room.

Chance did as he was told, and took a seat near the door, his tail flapping against the carpeted floor.

Darius unlocked the door and opened it.

On the other side, Eve stood, carrying a bottle of wine. She smiled. "Hi."

He let his eyes sweep over her curves in the long flowing green sundress she wore. The thin straps bared the tempting nooks of her neck and shoulders, and the gold sandals revealed her bright pink toenails.

"Hi. Come on in." Stepping aside, he let her enter his apartment.

She placed the bottle of wine on the kitchen counter, then stooped down to stroke Chance's head. "You must be Chance," she cooed. "Nice to meet you, boy."

The golden retriever licked her hand with appreciation,

and Darius smiled at their interaction. Within seconds, she'd already won Chance over. "Come on in the living room and have a seat."

With a gentle hand on the small of her back, he guided her to the sofa, where they both sat down.

She kicked off her sandals, tucking her pink toenails underneath her shapely bottom. "So, what movie are we watching?"

He smiled as he used the remote to change the channel. "Well, since you told me you liked jazz, I thought we'd watch a biography of one of the greatest."

She leaned toward him, her cocoa eyes sparkling with interest. "Really?"

"Yep. It's *Lady Sings the Blues*." He switched the television to the correct channel as the movie began.

She moved closer to him, snuggling into his side. "Oh, I love this movie. I haven't seen it in years."

He held her close, and settled in to watch the film.

When it ended, she wiped away the tears streaming down her beautiful brown cheeks with the back of her hand. "That movie always gets me," she whispered.

He dashed away a wayward tear with his finger. "Don't worry about it. Your compassion is part of what makes you so…beautiful." He punctuated the last word by touching his lips to hers.

When he pulled away, she looked up at him, her shining eyes filled with wonder. "You are amazing. When you kiss me like that—I can't even think straight."

He chuckled. "Good. I wouldn't want that pesky thinking getting in the way of this…" He pulled her closer and kissed her again. Feeling her lips part, he searched the depths of her mouth with his tongue, drawing the sweetness from her until she groaned beneath his lips.

"What?" he asked, his voice as soft as his heart for her. "Do you want to tell me something?"

Much to his amusement, she fanned herself with a hand. Taking a deep breath, she said. "Yes, I do. I wanted to ask you to be my escort to the launch party for MyBusiness Sapphire."

He thought for a moment. "Really? Don't you think that will complicate things?"

"I don't care. I'm going to be with you, regardless of what the board says." She stroked his cheek, batting her eyelashes. "You will go with me, won't you?"

He smiled at her false coyness. "Sure. I'm assuming I need a tuxedo for this party." He wasn't a fan of tuxedos. Black tie was rarely required when he was relaxing at his beach house or traveling for pleasure.

She nodded. "You knew the CEO job would involve stuff like this, right?"

He'd known something like this was coming, but he'd hoped to put off the stuffy side of the job for as long as possible. "Yes. I'll take care of it Monday." He ran a caressing hand over her bare shoulders. "Is that all you wanted to talk about?"

The blush filled her cheeks again. "I—suppose so."

"I've got something to tell you." He braced himself, because he had no idea how she would react to what he was about to say.

She looked at him expectantly.

"I'm giving up my position as CEO."

Her eyes widened. "What? Why?"

"Because the board is giving me hell about this, and I know you can handle the job. And, to be honest, I'm not the executive type." He gripped her shoulders gently. "This job was meant for you. It's what Mr. Franklin really wanted."

Her eyelids fluttered, as did the fan of dark lashes.

"Don't worry about me. I'm pretty eager to get back to enjoying my retirement."

She sighed, her gaze dropping to her lap. "I guess you've already made the decision, then."

"You can do this, Eve."

She looked unsure, but nodded. "I've been thinking about it." She stood, stretched. "If my mother and the board agree, then I'll do it."

"Good." He stood, drawing her by the hand to stand with him. "Then come with me."

"Where?"

He shook his head, loving her play at innocence. "To my bedroom. While you're still feeling adventurous." He pulled her into his arms again, and kissed her until he felt her shivering within his embrace.

He led her by the hand down the hallway, kicking the bedroom door shut behind them.

Chapter 19

Riding in the back of Eve's chauffeured car, Darius straightened his bow tie as they made their way to the ritzy Park Hotel for the launch party of FTI's new software. As he watched the twinkling lights of the Charlotte skyline glistening through the tinted window, he drew a deep, steadying breath.

Please, God, don't let me embarrass myself in front of these people.

Turning away from the window, he let his eyes sweep over her again. She held a small, lighted mirror compact in front of her face as she freshened her lipstick. She looked radiant tonight: the shimmering silver halter gown she wore hugged her curves in all the right places. Her upswept hair and smoky eyes gave her the look of the sophisticated, classy woman she was. He resisted the urge to lick his lips. "You look so beautiful tonight."

Closing the compact, she smiled his way. "Thank you, Darius. You know, that's the third time you've told me that since we picked you up."

"I know. But when you look that good, it bears repeating."

She reached out, stroking his clean-shaven cheek. "You look mighty handsome yourself, Mr. Winstead." She adjusted the silver bow tie he'd chosen to coordinate with her dress. "I think I just might have the most handsome escort in the room tonight."

Her gentle touch and kind words soothed his nerves. "I don't know about all that, but thanks for the compliment."

As she placed the compact back in her handbag, he watched her with appreciative, hungry eyes. *What a woman.*

The ride soon came to an end, as the sedan pulled into the crowded parking lot adjacent to the Park. The driver opened his door. Darius stepped out into the crisp night air, then went around to the other side of the vehicle to help Eve out.

With an enchanting femininity, she took his extended hand and moved out of the limo, pulling her silk wrap around her shoulders. She gave a nod to the driver, and he stepped back, allowing Darius to escort his beautiful girlfriend toward the open glass doors of the hotel.

As they crossed the courtyard to the door, he couldn't help noticing all the limousines and dark sedans pulling in to deposit their important, well-attired passengers. A sea of people in tuxedos and fancy gowns moved in the same direction. Looking around at the crowd made him glad he'd relinquished the CEO position. He was a blue-jeans kind of guy, and he'd hate to have to fancy up like this too often.

Taking his mind off the crowd, he turned his focus back to getting inside the hotel with the stunning woman on his arm. They entered through the open door, and a black-coated hotel employee showed them to the main ballroom.

The ballroom buzzed with combined voices of a thousand conversations, and the soft sound of classical piano being piped into the room. Black-coated waiters drifted through the field of white-clothed tables, passing trays of appetizers.

The exquisitely decorated space was quite a sight, but paled in comparison to Eve.

"We have a table reserved at the front." She was already weaving through the tables. "Come on. I'm sure Mom's waiting."

He followed her toward their aforementioned seats.

Without warning, she stopped dead in her tracks. He backed up a few steps to keep from crashing into her. "What is it? Do you see someone you know?"

"Unfortunately."

Surprised by her sudden contempt for this unseen person, he followed her gaze, until it landed on the well-dressed black man coming their way. The stranger pulled a petite Hispanic woman along by the hand.

Darius rolled his eyes. *This ought to be interesting.*

The man and his tiny companion came to a stop a few feet from them. "Eve, it's so lovely to see you again." He approached as if he were going to hug her.

Darius stepped into the space between Eve and the "fancy man." "Whoa. Back up there, brotherman."

The expensive suit looked at Darius with cold eyes, as if he'd just noticed him. "I'm sorry. Who are you?"

Eve stepped forward. "He's my date, Jeffrey."

Jeffrey snorted. "Oh, you mean this is your new boyfriend?" He looked Darius up and down, his beady little eyes filled with malice. "And to think you could have been with me."

She snapped, "But thank God I had better sense than that."

Jeffrey frowned. "Why are you so hostile, Eve? You should really be more open-minded. Rosie is." He looked down at his vapid, smiling date.

Having at least six inches and fifty pounds on the dude,

Darius clenched his fist. "And you really need to get away from us before I stuff your girl's purse down your throat."

Jeffrey stepped back. "There's no need for that 'street' attitude."

Angered by his insinuation, Darius jumped at the pompous little man.

Startled, Jeffrey flinched. Then, without another word, he dragged his date away.

Darius shook his head. "How do you know that guy?"

Eve sighed. "He took me on a date months ago. Big mistake. Let's just forget about him and enjoy the evening, okay?"

He straightened his bow tie and took her arm once again, content to forget about Mr. Short and Mouthy and enjoy the night.

She spotted her mother at their reserved table. "There's Mom." She gestured, and they made their way to where Louise was seated.

Mrs. Franklin wore a tasteful, well-cut black gown, and looked every bit the reigning matriarch of Franklin Technologies.

Eve's mother stood, and the two women embraced. "You look lovely tonight, dear," Louise said.

"Thanks, Mom. You look great, too." Eve stepped away from her mother, and turned to Darius.

He chimed in. "You look lovely this evening."

Louise's eyes lit with mischief. "Why, if I were twenty years younger, I'd…"

Eve giggled. "Mother."

Louise laughed. "Just kidding."

Watching Darius and her mother laughing and talking, Eve smiled to herself. She knew he was uncomfortable, but he was doing just fine. Besides, he didn't need to impress any of them to marry her.

As that thought crossed her mind, she blinked. Where had that come from? They had admitted their feelings for each other, but who knew where the road would lead?

For now, she decided it would be best if she turned her thoughts away from the distracting prospect of becoming Mrs. Darius Winstead. Instead, she focused on her speech.

Reaching into her silver sequined clutch, she pulled out the lavender note cards she'd brought, displaying the key points of her speech. Flipping through them, she thought about her father.

More than anything, she wished he could be there.

The launch party for MyBusiness Sapphire was planned months ago, when he'd still been in good health. Back then, he was the one slated to make the keynote address.

So many things had changed since then. She would give anything to hear her father's words of wisdom and encouragement right now.

"I know, baby. I miss him, too." Her mother's voice broke into her thoughts.

No words were needed, she just nodded in her mother's direction, and tried her best to concentrate on the words on her note cards.

Satisfied that she'd gone over her notes well enough, she allowed herself to take in the sights and sounds of the ballroom. It looked as if the Park staff spent hours decorating the large room. The white tablecloths provided a perfect backdrop for the tall, grandiose floral arrangements of dainty peonies, tall larkspur and bold yellow roses. Every detail, down to the polished silverware and the platinum-rimmed ivory china plates, had been carried out with painstaking detail. A look around was all it took for her to understand why her father insisted on having all FTI functions there.

Two other occupants soon joined their table of three. Mimi arrived first, and Eve almost didn't recognize her. She looked beautiful in the burgundy, high-collar dress with dragon motif she wore. Her dark, back-length hair was swept up into a high ponytail. As she took her seat between Eve and her mother, Eve complimented her taste.

Irvin arrived last. The security chief looked very handsome in his black tuxedo with red vest and bow tie. He took his seat with a bright smile.

"Decided to drop my serious demeanor, just for the night."

Waiters navigated the sea of tables, distributing the night's dinner. She admired the presentation of the grilled mesquite filet, spinach-kale sauté and potatoes au gratin set before her. Thanking the server, she sipped from her water glass. "So, Darius, how do you like the party so far?"

His smile traveled up to his dark brown eyes. "It's great. I can't wait to hear your speech, baby."

She stroked his cheek with her fingertips before returning her focus to her meal.

Throughout the meal, she and the other occupants of the table enjoyed an easygoing conversation. Even as she spoke, she couldn't help noticing the heated glances Darius kept shooting her way.

The lights in the ballroom lowered as Joel Kirk, FTI's chief marketing officer, crossed the raised stage to stand behind the podium. The din of conversations in the room softened to a hush as he cleared his throat.

"Ladies and gentlemen, on behalf of our CEO, Miss Eve Franklin, and the hardworking people at Franklin Technologies, Incorporated, I'd like to welcome you to our celebration of the latest in business management software, MyBusiness Sapphire."

Gasps of shock filled the room, followed by applause. A smiling Joel then began to speak again. "We are proud to bring you the best in office optimization software. Tonight, you'll learn all about our new product, and we'd like to get things started with a presentation from our chief technology officer, Ms. Li Sing Cho."

Joel began the applause as Li Sing, in an elegant navy blue floor-length sheath, made her way to the podium. As Li Sing introduced herself to the gathering, a white projection screen lowered behind her. Within moments, she launched into a presentation highlighting the many other benefits of the company's new software product.

When Li Sing finished, Eve joined in the hearty applause as she exited the stage. Joel Kirk appeared on stage again.

"And now, without further ado," Joel began, "I present to you the woman of the hour." He extended his hand toward her table in a dramatic manner. "Our illustrious CEO, Ms. Eve Franklin."

Thunderous applause filled the air as she rose from the table, and carefully made her way up the three steps to the stage. As she crossed to the podium, she shook hands with Joel, who left the stage promptly.

Looking out at the darkened room, she could make out a few faces, including Darius, who sat just below her. Taking a deep breath, she glanced at her first card and began to speak.

Darius watched Eve with rapt arousal as she stood at the podium, looking more poised and elegant than he'd ever seen her. As she spoke, her words captivated him like a siren's song.

"Good evening, everyone. Thank you all so much for coming out tonight. As Joel already pointed out, I took over as CEO effective yesterday. I'm fully prepared to carry my father's vision for FTI into the future." She paused, letting the applause rise, then die down. "Now, on with the reason we're here. MyBusiness Sapphire is just the first in a line of brilliant office optimization software products that we at Franklin Technologies plan to release. Let me take this time to congratulate Ms. Li Sing Cho, and all the hard-working people in the research and development department for making this possible."

She paused for applause, then spoke again once it faded. "I know that a lot of you knew my father. After he passed away, some at FTI spoke about canceling tonight's festivities." She paused, her eyes glistening with tears.

Seeing the wetness in her eyes tore at his heart. He did his best to project his strength to her, hoping it would buoy her.

She gathered herself, continued. Eve spoke about her parent's acquisition of the company, and the accomplishments her father made during his tenure as CEO. She smiled a watery smile. "I miss him terribly, I must admit. But the accomplishments that he made in his life should be celebrated, and that's why we are here tonight."

Around the ballroom, people began to stand and clap. Soon, the room's occupants rose in a full-on standing ovation. Moved by her words of praise for her father, Darius stood and cheered right along with them. Exuding grace from her beautiful smile, she stood on the stage until the thunderous sound dimmed.

"Thank you so much. And now, I have some wonderful news to share." Reaching down onto a hidden shelf in the podium, she produced a piece of paper. "This is a declaration that I've had drawn up. In loving memory of my father, I have donated $250,000 to create the Joseph Tyler Franklin Memorial Scholarship Fund at Johnson C. Smith University. Each year, thirty-five deserving students majoring in computer science or information technology will receive this scholarship, which covers their tuition and fees."

Louise emitted an emotional gasp, clasping her hand over her mouth, as the applause once again filled the ballroom. Darius shook his head in disbelief.

Once again, she'd surprised him with the sweetness in her soul. He vowed then and there to spend the rest of the night showing her just how amazing she was.

Curtsying and waving, she walked off the stage with the sounds of appreciation still filling the room. As she approached the table, her mother stood. He saw the tears standing in Louise's eyes as she embraced her daughter.

"I'm so proud of you, Eve," Louise whispered in a voice trembling with emotion. "And your father would be, too."

Pulling away, she nodded, dashing away the tears running down her own cheeks. "I hope so, Mom."

Darius slid out her chair, and she sat down. Returning to his seat next to her, he whispered for her ears only. "I love you, Eve Franklin."

Without hesitation, she turned to him and replied, "I love you, Darius."

He stroked her tear-dampened cheek, his heart swelling in his chest.

Now that he knew she was truly his, he vowed to always treat her like the queen she was.

The rest of the evening went by, but not fast enough for him. He couldn't take his eyes off Eve. But she returned his gaze, which communicated to him all the things she couldn't say in the public setting.

As they rode in the back of the chauffeured vehicle,

they held each other close, whispering and necking like hormone-crazed teenagers. By the time they arrived at her house, she'd taken off her heels, and he'd pulled all the pins from her hair, freeing it to fall around her shoulders.

As the car pulled away from the front of the house, they embraced. With her shoes in one hand, she led him down a cobblestone path around the side of the house.

"Where are we going?" he asked, curious.

"You'll see."

In a few moments, they had rounded the house. In the back of the property sat an oak gazebo, illuminated by the moonlight. Dark, burgundy-hued roses climbed the sides, and a small garden surrounded the sturdy-looking structure.

As she pulled him up the stairs, she flopped down on the cushioned bench that bordered the interior of the gazebo. "Come sit with me." She beckoned with a graceful finger.

Her soulful eyes and the sequined bodice of her dress glistened in the faint light. He did as she asked, and joined her on the seat.

Their eyes locked.

Time slowed.

His hands, of their own accord, undid the clasp of her halter neck gown.

She didn't resist as he pulled the top of the gown aside, revealing the tempting mounds of her breasts to the crisp night air. He bent, taking one nipple between his lips. She shivered, a soft croon escaping her throat.

He kissed the flat plane between her breasts, nipped and savored the sweetness of her shoulders and the delicate crook of her neck. Her heavy breathing and quiet moans filled his ears and fired his blood. Desire raged inside him like a five alarm blaze. He was sure they could set off a smoke detector if there was one nearby.

He mused that when he made her his wife, he would take her here, with the moon shining down on her and the breeze caressing her skin…

With sure hands, he slid his hand up her leg, navigating around the split in her dress until he touched her thigh. The lacy edge of her panties slid underneath his fingertips. As she sighed, he pushed the fabric aside and plied the dampness sheltered there.

Her hips rose from the bench, and as he pulled her onto his lap, his lips crashed down onto hers. His tongue searched her sweet mouth, as his fingertips dipped into a paradise of a different kind. She already flowed sweet and warm, and he played her like the strings of his bass. Her thighs parted in greedy invitation.

He kept it up, kissing her lips and stroking her treasure, until she came, shaking and moaning and calling out his name like a melody on the night air.

Chapter 20

Driving toward FTI, Eve sat back in her seat, content. Darius called that morning, asking her if they could spend the evening together. She couldn't wait to get the day under way, because every passing hour brought her closer to Darius's sweet kisses and skillful caressing.

Just thinking of him brought back a flood of erotic memories. She couldn't believe she'd been celibate for two years. Now that she'd experienced what Darius offered, she was hungry for more.

Scandalized by her greediness for his loving, she decided to turn her thoughts to things less distracting. Turning up the smooth jazz on her radio, she bopped her head to the beat.

She exited the highway and turned into the heart of the city. People meandered up and down the street, talking on cell phones, sipping from paper coffee cups and waiting at bus stops. She gazed out the window, taking in the familiar sights of the city she'd been raised in. She guided her truck down Trade Street, nearing the FTI building. Traffic every morning in this area flowed like cold molasses, so she wasn't surprised when she was forced to slow down.

She crept along at an achingly slow pace for the next few minutes. Finally, things seemed to pick up. The cars ahead of them increased speed, and she did the same.

Arriving in front of the building, she slipped into her parking spot. Then she made her way across the crowded plaza toward the doors.

As she reached for the door, it swung open, almost knocking her down. She stepped back to allow the person to pass, and came face-to-face with a very smug-looking Phillip Gordon. Behind him was a short, balding man in a dark suit.

"There you are, Eve." Phillip's tone dripped contempt.

She smiled politely, even as she wondered why on earth he'd been looking for her. "Good morning, Phillip. Is there something I can do for you?"

"Meet Bertram Faulkner, my lawyer." Phillip gestured to the stout man behind him. "He has something for you."

As her brow knit in confusion, the lawyer handed her a piece of paper. "You've been summoned, ma'am."

"I told you this wasn't over." Phillip laughed venomously. "See you in court, Ms. Franklin." He and Faulkner marched past her, disappearing into the bustling crowd on the sidewalk

Annoyance coursed through her like a shot of espresso as she read the paper she'd been handed. Anger quickly replaced her annoyance, and she folded the paper in half and tucked it into her handbag. Fishing out her cell phone, she placed a call to Lina as she punched the elevator button.

"Hello?"

"Lina, get over here as soon as you can." She stepped into the elevator car, glad to be alone as the doors slid closed. "Phillip Gordon is suing me for wrongful termination."

She could hear Lina's groan. "I wish I could, but I'm at the courthouse. We're in a brief recess, then I'm back up. Can I swing by a little later?"

"I guess that will have to do. Thanks." Eve disconnected the call and leaned back against the wall of the elevator car.

* * *

Darius peered at the front entrance to the FTI building, waiting for Eve to appear. He'd been waiting there twenty minutes, and as the flood of employees leaving work for the day continued to flow out onto the sidewalk along Trade Street, he grew worried. What if she'd had a rough moment and was locked in her office, crying? Even though she'd displayed a lot of strength, he knew she still mourned her father. Or maybe she'd forgotten their rendezvous. He hoped that wasn't the case, especially after the loving they'd shared.

With a groan, he got out of the car and slammed the door behind him. Feeding several more quarters into the parking meter, he crossed the sidewalk and plaza and entered the building.

Scanning the lobby, he didn't see her in the group of people hanging around, so he went to the main reception desk. "Excuse me. Has Ms. Franklin left for the day?"

The petite blonde shook her head. "No. I believe she's still upstairs. Would you like me to ring her office?"

He shook his head. "No, thanks." Passing the desk, he headed for the elevator bank. He was reaching out to press the up button when the center elevator opened. Eve stepped off, her face an unreadable mask.

He smiled, hoping to lift her out of her apparent funk. "Hey, gorgeous. Ready for my surprise?"

She looked his way, as if just noticing him. To his surprise, her frown deepened. "No, Darius, I'm not. In fact, I think you've done quite enough already."

Taken aback by her tone and her words, he stepped back to allow her off the car. "Eve, what's wrong with you?"

She strode past him, as if she intended to ignore him.

Confused and irritated, he followed her. "Eve…"

"I don't want to talk to you right now, Darius." She

tossed the words over her shoulder in a terse tone, without even looking back as she swung open the glass door and stalked out.

His irritation increased tenfold as she made a show of walking away from him. On the plaza, he caught her arm with a gentle, but firm hold.

She turned to face him, her lips pursed into a scowl. But her eyes held something else. They were wet and red, and there was obvious sadness there. "Eve, you're not going to push me away with that funky attitude. Now, what is going on with you?"

Her eyes slid closed for a moment, and she blew out a long breath. "Phillip Gordon is suing me for wrongful termination."

He shook his head at the mention of the old blowhard's name. "What? Why?"

"You know why. I told you this would cause problems, but you insisted on pursuing me, anyway!" The tears were running down her cheeks now, and she pulled out of his grasp, backing away as she spoke.

His heart sank into his loafers. He remembered the promise Gordon had made the day he fired him, and supposed he shouldn't be surprised at this turn of events. Still, seeing Eve so upset did something to him.

"Wait a minute!" He matched her pace as she tried to slink away. "I left this company to avoid that, and so you could step into your rightful place here. How can you blame this on me?"

Arms folded across her chest, she shot back, "Easily. I can't believe I let myself get mixed up with a coworker." She shook her head, a bitter laugh escaping her throat.

"I don't work here anymore." He stared into her brown eyes, looking for a trace of the woman he'd come to love. "We're in this together, baby."

"No, we're not. I'm the only one getting sued."

She turned away as if to head for her car, but he caught her hand. He couldn't let her leave, not like this. Didn't she remember what they'd shared? "Don't turn your back on what we have, Eve. That's too much like Olivia." As soon as the words escaped, he groaned. It was the wrong thing to say, but now it was too late.

He heard her gasp. She looked up at him, her eyes holding a coldness he'd never seen there before. "Since what we have caused all this, it's better if I let you go."

Her blunt words left him stunned. Before he could formulate a response, she got into her truck. With a final, teary gaze, she started the engine and pulled away.

As he watched, his heart pounding like a congo drum in his ears, the truck pulled away from the curb and disappeared into the rush of evening traffic.

He stood there for a long moment, his breath coming in rapid spurts, clenching his fists at his sides. After all he'd done to prove how much he cared for her, she'd turned her back on him. Maybe she was more like Olivia than he'd thought.

He strode to his car, and once inside, he slammed the door. Starting the engine and blasting the radio, he waited for an opening in traffic, then sped off down Tryon Street.

Sitting behind her desk, Eve ceased the nervous tapping of her pencil on the desktop when Lina walked into the open doors of her office.

"Thanks for helping me out with this." She got up from her chair, and crossed to where Lina had sat down on the love seat in the sitting area.

"All right, first things first. Why aren't you using your company lawyers for this?" She opened her briefcase, shuffling through a stack of papers.

"It's sad to say, but I don't trust them." Eve folded her hands in her lap. "They've known and worked for Phillip Gordon for so many years, I'm afraid they may take his side in all this."

Lina nodded, crossing her legs. "I see. I've been handling more union cases than anything else lately, so I wouldn't mind taking a side trip into the exciting world of dismissal law." She looked up from the papers long enough to give Eve an exaggerated wink. "As a favor to you, of course."

She found herself smiling despite her mood. Between being nervous about the hearing and being tense by thoughts of Darius, she needed the lift. "I appreciate it. So, what do you have for me?"

Lina handed her some papers and a silver metallic pen. "Just my standard retainer, and some forms the firm will want filled out. Once you finish that, we can jump into this thing headfirst."

She took the offered papers and pen and began reading the documents. After she'd signed and initialed in all the indicated places, she passed it all back to Lina, who tucked it into her briefcase. "I can tell you right now that Gordon's case is flimsy, at best. I'm almost surprised any lawyer would take the case on."

Hearing that gave her a measure of comfort, and she sighed. "That's good to hear. What I really want to know is, what's our defense?"

Lina leaned back into the cushion, tapping the tip of the pen on her chin. "In a case like this, it's more like presenting the facts than mounting a defense. The burden of proof is on him and his lawyer."

She nodded, knowing Lina was about to slip into legalese. "So, do you really think his case is invalid?"

"Was he the only person who was fired, promoted or

who changed positions? In other words, was he singled out?"

"No. There were a good number of promotions and job changes as well, after Dad got sick." She could clearly remember how crazy those days were.

Lina pointed the pen at her. "See? We can argue that Phillip Gordon's firing was really just part of a larger trend of reorganization within the company."

Turning it over in her mind, she could see the validity of her friend's point. "Sounds great. What happens now?"

"We'll get a hearing on the schedule and hash this thing out in front of a judge. Bada-bing, bada-boom, it should be over. Although—" She looked away, as if avoiding a topic.

Her eyebrow went up. "Although, what?"

"Wasn't Darius the one who did the actual firing?"

The mention of his name stung like the bite of a very large mosquito. "Yes. He was in the CEO position at the time."

"It would be beneficial to have him there. The judge may have questions for him."

She winced. "I don't think he wants to hear from me right now, and I can't say I'm all that interested in talking to him."

Lina's expression became curious. "Why not? What's going on with you two?"

"We're not speaking."

"And why is that?"

She rolled her eyes. "Come on, Lina. This whole lawsuit mess is his fault."

Lina's brow furrowed, her lips pursed. In a word, she looked unconvinced. "And how did you come to that conclusion?" She crossed her legs and waited.

She didn't care for the way her friend had put her on the spot. "It's just like I told him. If he hadn't insisted on pursuing me while we were working together, Phillip wouldn't have gotten riled up, and this would have never happened."

Lina scoffed. "How do you know that? Didn't you tell me that you and Gordon never got along? I'm sure he would have found some other way to make things difficult for you, if this hadn't gone down."

She hadn't considered that, but to her mind, it didn't change a thing. "Well, Lina, it is what it is. Now that he's back to enjoying his early retirement, he gets to avoid the whole situation while I'm forced to deal with it."

"No, he doesn't. I just told you he'll need to be in court, in case the judge has questions." Lina fixed a serious gaze on her. "But why are you really giving him such a hard time?"

"I told you. This whole thing is his fault." She stood, going to the minifridge to get a soda. After popping the top on a can of ginger ale, she took a long sip. When she turned back around, she found Lina still staring her down. "What do you want from me?"

"The truth, but I'm not about to get it today." Lina shook her head and stood. "I'm going back to my office to prepare for the hearing. I'll contact Darius. It's my job as your legal counsel." Gathering up her briefcase and purse, she started to walk out, but paused in the doorway. "And as your friend, it's my job to tell you that if you let him go, you would be a damn fool."

Before Eve could swallow her drink and shout a retort, Lina was gone.

Chapter 21

Darius scanned the small courtroom, looking for an open seat. Only a few were left, near the back, as the room only held about twenty or so seats to begin with. Straightening his solid red tie and brushing a bit of lint from his black suit, he slipped down the back row to an empty chair.

He'd received a call from Lina a little over a week ago, asking him to be present at the hearing on Phillip Gordon's wrongful termination suit. He understood why his being there was important. What he didn't get was why Lina had called him, instead of Eve. He knew she was frustrated and angry at being sued, anyone would be. Taking it all out on him, however, still seemed petty and downright unreasonable. Part of him had wanted to stay home and let her handle this alone, but he didn't want her to go down in flames over this. In a way, their relationship had played a role in getting to this point, so he would shoulder some of the blame. He would not, however, accept complete responsibility.

The past week and a half without her had been hell. He'd woken at night, expecting her to be cuddled up next to him, only to realize he was alone, hard and aching for her. Visions of her smiling face, her shapely body and the sound of her calling his name haunted his dreams. He'd had enough of being separated from her, and he planned to tell her that, as soon as this thing was over.

After he took his seat, he glanced at the front of the room, where two tables faced a bench. It was the typical setup for a case not being heard by a jury—he'd seen enough court proceedings on television to know that. At the right table, he could see Eve and Lina talking in hushed tones. At the left table, Phillip Gordon and his lawyer were simply sitting, as if waiting for a show to begin. He couldn't help noticing the smug-looking grin on Phillip's face, and he truly wished he could get up and slap the taste right out of his mouth. Knowing that would probably result in assault charges, he sat back in his chair and waited for the proceedings to begin.

A black-robed woman, with fiery red hair and pale skin, climbed up onto the seat at the bench. "I'll hear the next case now."

The bailiff called out the case number and the particulars, then stepped back into the front corner of the room.

"Counsel Faulkner, state your business." The judge eyed the short, balding lawyer from her seat.

"Your Honor, my client, Phillip Gordon, has been the victim of a grievous injustice. He was wrongfully and spitefully terminated from his position as chief operations officer at Franklin Technologies, Incorporated. All of this was due to the uncouth fraternization occurring between two board members, and Mr. Gordon would like to be duly compensated for his loss of income and mental anguish."

Darius snorted a laugh. As a few people turned back to look in his direction, he attempted to cover his gesture with a cough. He knew court proceedings were a serious matter, but he couldn't have held back that laugh if he'd wanted to. Mental anguish? Uncouth fraternization? What was Gordon's lawyer drinking before he showed up in court? It must have been some strong liquor, because he was just throwing around a bunch of big words over what was obviously a small matter.

After Faulkner sat down, the judge gestured to Lina. "Counsel Smith-Todd, please."

Lina stood and walked to the center of the room, directly in front of the bench. Her navy pantsuit, pulled-back hair and the set of her jaw conveyed her seriousness as well as her professionalism. "Your Honor, my client is the victim here. The victim of an embittered man and an overly litigious society. Eve Franklin is not the kind of person to terminate an employee based on petty, childish disagreements. Today, I'm going to prove that Mr. Gordon's termination, while unfortunate, was simply part of a larger restructuring effort taking place at Franklin Technologies. It was a necessary process following the serious illness of the founder and CEO. I hope not to monopolize much of the court's time today, as I'm sure you have cases to hear that have actual merit." With a sly smile on her face, Lina strode back to the table and took her seat.

Looking back to Faulkner and Gordon, Darius could see that the two old men were damn near breathing fire. Both of their faces displayed the fact that they did not like being put in their place, especially by a woman. He smiled to himself, silently giving Lina props as he continued to watch the proceedings.

The rest of the hearing went by in a blur of legal talk and back-and-forth. Lina remained calm the entire time, but Faulkner continuously looked as if his head would explode at any moment. He didn't know Lina that well, but seeing her in action in the courtroom left him impressed.

The judge interjected in the middle of one of Faulkner's drawn-out speeches. "Mr. Faulkner, please. I've heard enough."

Looking put out, Faulkner closed his mouth and sat.

The judge continued. "I'm told Ms. Franklin didn't do the actual firing. That was done by the acting CEO..." She looked down at a piece of paper in front of her. "Darius Winstead. Is he present?"

Upon hearing his name, he stood. "Here I am, Your Honor."

"I've only one question for you, Mr. Winstead. What was your reasoning for firing Mr. Gordon?"

He recalled the events of the day clearly, and didn't hesitate in his answer. "Insubordination. Mr. Gordon was extremely disrespectful to both myself and Ms. Franklin. I reprimanded him twice before his dismissal. As a matter of fact, on the day in question, Mr. Gordon referred to me as 'boy.'"

A murmur of whispers went through the room. The judge banged her gavel to silence the din. "Thank you, Mr. Winstead."

He sat back down. He looked Eve's way, and found her watching him. When their eyes met, hers fled. Even as she avoided his gaze, he smiled. Deep down, he knew she would come around.

The judge cleared her throat. "Well, I've heard more than I care to hear on this case, so I'll make my ruling now. Mr. Gordon, in the future, if you want to hold on to your job, don't go around insulting your superiors. North Carolina is an at-will state, where either party can terminate employment for any reason, or no reason, at any time. The only exception is in cases that violate state or federal laws, or are discriminatory in nature. No such exception has occurred here, which I'm sure Counsel Faulkner would have known had he recently cracked a law book open."

Gordon's lawyer looked properly chastised.

The judge stood, banging her gavel. "Case dismissed."

Lina and Eve shared a hug, as Gordon shouted and raged at his attorney. Eventually, the two red-faced men made their way out of the room.

As the room emptied, Darius watched Lina whisper something in Eve's ear, then gather her things and slip out a door near the front of the courtroom. At that point, he and Eve were the only two people left standing in the room. He stood, eyes locked on hers, and strolled in her direction.

Eve could see Darius coming her way, and looked around for an escape route. Having never been to this part of the courthouse before, she only knew one way out—the way she'd come in, which she'd have to pass him to get to. Seeing him, looking more handsome than he had any right to in a dark suit and red tie, made her think of the past nine nights she'd spent without him. He'd become a fixture in her world, a solid, steady, safe thing to cling to when life became storm tossed. Not speaking to him for so long had made her realize just how lonely she'd been before he'd stepped into the elevator car, and into her life.

Sighing, she resigned herself to taking Lina's whispered advice: she would stop running from him and deal with her feelings once and for all.

He approached her, but stayed back a few steps, as if he thought she might slap him. "Eve."

It was just a single word, but her name on his lips was one of the most pleasant sounds she'd ever heard. "Darius."

He watched her, his gaze intense. "Don't you have something to say to me?"

She rolled her eyes, then pursed her lips. "Would Olivia apologize to you?"

He leaned back a bit, his hand to his heart. "Ouch."

She crossed her arms over her chest. "If you don't like

the sound of that, think about how I felt being compared to her."

He cast his eyes down for a moment, then held her gaze with a sincerity that touched her. "You're right. I never should have said that, and I'm sorry." His eyes now held genuine remorse. "Can you forgive me?"

She inhaled deeply. "If you can forgive me. I should never have blown up at you about the lawsuit. I was just so pissed off about the whole thing."

He came closer, reaching for her. She went into his arms without hesitation. His warm breath on the lobe of her ear, he whispered, "I forgive you, my love."

His words sent heat flooding through her veins, and her knees buckled beneath her. Forgetting that they were in the Mecklenburg County Courthouse, standing before the judge's bench, she raised her chin to his kiss and let herself be swept away. His lips were hot, forceful and tantalizing as he kissed away the loneliness she'd felt in the previous days.

Only the loud clearing of someone's throat made him break the contact.

Turning around, she saw the bailiff, arms folded, standing in the doorway near the bench. "Take it outside, kids. We've got other cases to hear."

Heat rushing to her cheeks, she picked up her purse from the table and gestured to Darius with her index finger. "You heard the man. Let's get out of here."

He chuckled. "After you."

She grabbed his hand, and pulled him down the aisle and through the door at the rear of the room.

Outside, she let him lead her to his car. The ride to his house was the longest, hottest trip she'd ever taken. As he navigated the city streets with his left hand, he kept his right hand on her. His fingertips slipped beneath the hem of her tan skirt, stroking the delicate flesh of her thigh. She lay back in the seat, breathless with desire for him, as he brushed his knuckle against the damp spot on her panties. By the time they arrived at his town house, she was moist, pulsing and on the verge of orgasm. The man was good with his hands in a way that blew her mind.

Getting into his place was a frenzy of kissing, fiddling for the keyhole and pushing their way inside, all while locked together. They parted momentarily to avoid stepping on Chance as they made a beeline for the bedroom.

He pressed her against the wall, and she could feel his hardness jutting between her thighs. He was ready, and so was she. She put up no protest as he removed her jacket, blouse and bra, tossing them to the floor. Then he stripped her skirt and panties down her hips, leaving her naked except for her thigh-high panty hose and beige pumps.

He stopped for a moment, staring at her with hot, glittering eyes. Running his hands over her hard, pulsing nipples, he stepped back for a moment to grab a condom from his nightstand. As she watched, still leaning against the wall, he snatched off his clothes and sheathed his manhood with the protection.

He lifted her into his arms, still pressing her back against the wall, and kissed her with such intensity, she trembled. Her legs wrapped around his waist on their own, as if they were always meant to be there. As the kiss deepened, their tongues mating and dancing in an age-old rhythm, he tilted her hips and plunged inside her, drawing a long moan from her throat.

Time stood still, and the world slipped away, as he filled her again and again, his powerful hips rocking back and forth. She could hear her own moans of pleasure echoing in her head, as well as his heavy breathing, as he took her to a place only lovers could reach. His mouth left hers to place kisses on her brow, her eyes and her neck. When he drew a nipple into his hot mouth and suckled, she came, crying and twisting against him as waves of ecstasy shook her to her very core.

He continued his sweet torture, driving into her until his own release grabbed him. He then groaned her name aloud, grinding his hips until she felt he would permanently pin her to the wall.

When she came back to full awareness, he was laying her down on his bed, the mattress giving beneath their combined weight. She wanted to kiss him, to tell him how much she loved him, but before the words could be formed, she slipped into a sated sleep.

Chapter 22

Adjusting the hem of her midnight blue cocktail dress for a final time, Eve walked into the Blue. The lure of the Gents' live music always seemed to draw a lot of people.

Sidestepping and maneuvering, she made her way to her usual table, a few feet in front of the stage. Lina already waited there, waving wildly, as if Eve didn't see her.

She slid into the seat next to Lina. "Okay, what's going on? I know you know something."

Lina cut her a sly look. "I don't know what you're talking about. Lighten up and enjoy yourself. We're all celebrating your victory, so just go with it." Patting Eve on the shoulder, Lina turned back to the stage.

Knowing she wasn't going to get any more information out of her friend, Eve sighed and took a look around her. To her surprise, other familiar faces occupied tables nearby. Mimi and Irvin sat at one, and oddly enough, some of the other staff members from FTI were sprinkled through the club's interior.

Assuming Lina was being honest, they were all there to celebrate the dismissal of Phillip Gordon's lawsuit. Shrugging, she focused her attention ahead.

The announcer stepped out onto the stage and grabbed the microphone from the stand. "Welcome, ladies and gentlemen, to the Blue Lounge's Wednesday Night Jazz Flight.

We hope you enjoy the jazzy sounds of Charlotte's own Queen City Gents." He paused as applause filled the air.

As the announcer left the stage, the heavy blue curtain rose to reveal the band. The house lights dropped, and the stage lights illuminated the four men, stationed behind their respective instruments.

She watched them for a moment before she realized they wore tuxedos and silver bow ties. *This is going to be some party.* She smiled to herself at all the fuss everyone made over her.

Rashad spoke into the microphone sitting atop the grand piano. "That's right, y'all. The Gents are in the house, and it's a party!" His fingers glided over the keys, playing the opening notes of a song. His eyes met hers. "Eve, we're glad to see you doing your thing."

The band launched into a rousing, upbeat set. They flowed easily through classics by the Duke and Ira Gershwin. Then Marco got to show off as they moved into some songs made popular by contemporary smooth jazz saxophonist Eric Darius.

The space between the tables came alive with swaying bodies dancing to the music. Even Louise and Irvin hit the floor, and Eve couldn't hide her surprise as she watched them cut a rug together. She hadn't initially noticed her mother's presence, and seeing Louise so carefree made Eve smile.

"Wow. Mom's got rhythm!" Eve giggled at the sight.

Louise shouted, "Of course I do!"

Lina was also amused by the sight. "Whoa! Go on with your bad self, Louise!"

Eve laughed out loud, feeling a peace in her heart that she hadn't felt in weeks. Here, surrounded by the sounds of good music, and enjoying the company of the people she loved, everything seemed right. The pain of losing her father would probably be with her for the rest of her life, but having people like Lina and her mother around her lessened it.

As the set drew to a close, Eve watched the band take their bows. They left the stage quietly, but to her surprise, Darius remained. He stood alone as the blue curtain lowered, illuminated by a single spotlight.

His eyes locked with hers, he began to speak. "Ladies and gentlemen, I'd like to say a few words about the lady in my life, Ms. Eve Franklin."

Eve could feel hot tears cascading down her cheeks. Looking at her mother, she saw her crying, as well.

He continued talking, but now he made his way off the stage and toward the table where she sat. The spotlight followed him. "No other woman ever filled my life with such love and happiness. Now I want to return the favor, by spending the rest of my life making her glad she's alive."

He stopped at her table, and knelt before her seat. Glancing at Lina, who wore a wide grin, she turned back to look into his eyes, and saw all the affection displayed in them.

He reached into his jacket pocket, and produced a small blue box. Opening it, he revealed a huge princess cut diamond on a yellow gold band. "Eve Yoruba Franklin, will you be my wife?"

Her eyes so full of water she could barely see, she nodded briskly. When he continued to wait for a response, she shouted, "Yes!"

The room erupted into wild applause and cheering as he slid the ring onto her finger. Gathering her into his arms, he stood her up. And right there, in front of everyone, he kissed her as if to brand her his forever.

Darius opened the microwave door to cease its beeping. The smell of extra-butter microwave popcorn filled his apartment. Grasping the edge of the bag, he took it out, closing the door. Once he'd filled a large plastic bowl from his cabinet with the steaming kernels, he took the short journey from the kitchen to the living room, where Eve lay stretched out on the sofa.

Setting the bowl down on the coffee table, he let his eyes travel her bare legs, revealed by the khaki shorts she wore. Her bright red toenails were propped up on the arm of the couch. "Excuse me." He grabbed her legs, pushed them aside, and took a seat.

She tossed a pillow at him. "Hey, I was comfortable."

"I could see that." He sipped from the glass of Pepsi he'd left sitting on the table. "But I needed somewhere to sit." He leaned close to her, stroked her jaw. "I'll make it worth your while."

With desire sparkling in her cocoa eyes, she kissed his forehead. "Naughty boy. I thought you asked me over to watch television and chill out."

"That doesn't mean we can't heat things up a little later."

She giggled. "Are you going to be okay until the show goes off, or do I need to douse you with Pepsi to cool you off?"

Rolling his eyes, he turned toward the television. Listening to the announcer describe the show, and seeing the images roll by, he turned wide eyes on her. "*World's Stupidest Stunts*? This is what you want to watch?"

She propped herself up on her elbow. "What can I say, I like watching stupid people get hurt sometimes."

He shook his head. He'd never known a sister who liked watching a guy take a blow to the family jewels, or at least not one who would admit it. "You should watch *SportsCenter* with me. There's plenty of carnage to be seen in the highlights during football season. Not to mention NASCAR crashes, UFC knockouts, the whole nine."

Chance, who'd been lying between the coffee table and the couch, raised his head. Just as he made a play for the popcorn bowl, Eve snatched it up. "No, Chance."

Looking very guilty, Chance slid under the table, his paws over his snout.

Darius shook his head. *Wish I could always get him to do what I say.*

Stuffing a handful of popcorn into his mouth, he sat back, pulling her legs into his lap.

The show proved hilarious. Watching idiotic skateboarders render themselves sterile while trying to do tricks on handrails, and seeing other fools take blows to various parts of the body, he laughed harder than he had in weeks. Their bad judgment was his entertainment.

Looking over at her, he saw her laughing so hard she wiped away tears. The fit of laughter caused her tempting breasts to bounce subtly. Watching her suddenly became much more appealing than the picture on the TV.

She looked at him, her eyes sparkling with dampness. "What? Why are you staring at me like that?"

He said nothing. Instead, he leaned over and pulled her into his arms. Lacing his fingers in her red-streaked hair, he brought her forward for his kiss. Her lips were yielding and soft, and the sultry croon that escaped from her throat spurred him on.

As the kiss deepened, he stroked her shoulders and the scented expanse of her throat.

Looking at her, all he could think about was laying her down and making love to her until she called his name.

She pulled away, panting as if breathless. "Darius—good grief." She fanned herself with her hand. "If you wanna see the rest of this, you'd better quit."

He grazed his thumb over her right nipple, enjoying the way it stiffened under his touch. "The choice is yours."

Her eyes slid closed, and she let him continue talking to her body with his hands. Each part of her responded in kind, answering his sensual call.

A pounding at his front door interrupted the moment. With a curse, Darius went to the door. "Who is it?"

No one answered, so he looked through the peephole in the door.

"Who's out there?" She looked on curiously.

"Nobody." He couldn't see anyone standing at the door, but he knew the knock hadn't been imagined. "Unless it's somebody really short."

To satisfy his own curiosity, he opened the door. No one was there, but there was something lying on the cement stoop outside his door. He flicked on the porch light, then stooped down to get a closer look.

She walked up behind him, circling her arms around his waist. "What is it?"

Looking at the object, his eyes widened. He picked it up, and stared in disbelief. "This can't be real. It's got to be a replica or something."

The object was a framed, autographed photo of Duke Ellington.

"Wow. If it's a fake, it's a very good one." She peered around his shoulder for a closer look. "It looks antique to me."

He studied the faded mahogany frame, with its hand-carved embellishments, and he had to agree. Turning the frame over, he saw a yellow Post-it note stuck to the back. Peeling it off carefully to not damage the frame, he read it aloud. "For Darius. Keep spreading the joy of jazz. The Music Man."

"Who in the world is the Music Man?" Her voice was filled with the awe he felt.

He looked off into the night, his eyes scanning for any sign of the person who'd left him something so grand. "I have no idea."

Chapter 23

Darius stood near the window of the Sunday school room he'd been confined to. Lina had come charging into the church about an hour ago, insisting he stay there so he wouldn't see Eve as she entered the building. He'd agreed, knowing Lina wasn't going to give him a choice. But he requested that he not be imprisoned alone. So, he, Rashad, Marco and Ken, along with his father, occupied the room together, waiting to be released.

The sun began to set outside, but Darius could still see people standing outside the front doors of the church. Some stopped to converse with friends, others rushed into the building. He turned toward the other men in the room, and found them all watching him intently. "What?"

Quincy spoke. "How are you feeling?"

He did his best impersonation of a pro baller's pregame stretch. "I'm ready, coach. Put me in the game."

Quincy chuckled. "Good. Keep that attitude."

Marco straightened his white bow tie. "Yeah. Just don't rip the tuxedo while you're expressing your 'readiness.'"

Darius came over to the table and took the vacant seat between his father and Ken.

Quincy turned to him, his eyes serious. "You're making a very big commitment, Darius. I wanted to marry Olivia, but she was a free spirit—too creative to be tied down."

He scoffed. "Creative? Don't you mean selfish?"

"Darius, she was selfish then. That's true. But people grow older, they change."

"Not Olivia. I bet she's the same way now." Darius slapped his palm on the table. "Why are we talking about her now, anyway?"

The creaking of the door caught his attention, and he turned toward the sound. To his shock, Olivia stepped into the room.

Rashad, whose wide eyes resembled two full moons, stood. "Gents, maybe we should make ourselves scarce."

Olivia closed the door behind her. "No, boys. Don't leave. I want you all to hear what I have to say to my son."

Rashad hesitated, then dropped back down into the chair.

Darius stood, staring at her with cold eyes. "Why are you here?"

She moved closer. "Because my only child is getting married, and I wanted to be here."

Quiet rage filled him. He wanted to throw something, but he knew better than to act so brusque in God's house. "Now you want to be here? You've missed my whole life up until now." He placed a hand to his now throbbing head. "Oh, wait, I take that back. You did show a while back, just long enough to insult the woman I'm about to marry."

Olivia's gaze lowered. She looked wounded by his comments. "I know you're angry with me, Darius. And you have every right to be." The tapping sound of her high-heeled shoes filled the otherwise silent room as she slowly approached him. "I haven't been the mother I should have been to you."

Darius turned away from her. Why was she really here? He didn't want to guess at her motives, so he came out and asked her. "Are you looking for money?"

"Darius, this isn't about money. If it was about money, I would have come years ago, when you sold your phone software thing."

That gave him pause. "You knew about that?"

"Of course. It was all over the news—a great accomplishment, especially for a young man. I was so proud of you."

He felt a tightness in his chest.

She brushed away a tear running down her cheek. "Look, I don't expect us to have a relationship right away. All I'm asking is that you give this a chance. Let's make today a starting point, okay?"

He turned back toward her, and found her brown eyes filled with remorse. How could she come here, on his wedding day, and disrupt everything?

Olivia's voice shook with emotion. "I'm sorry, Darius. For all the pain I've caused you and your father, I'm truly, truly sorry."

Darius noted that for the first time in his life, she'd admitted that she wasn't a good mother, and her guilt seemed genuine. He thought of his paternal grandmother, Ma Beaulah, sitting in the sanctuary right now. She'd always taught him that forgiveness wasn't for the person you forgave, but for you.

He could hear Ma Beaulah's words in his mind. *Hate and bitterness will consume you if you don't forgive folks. Don't give nobody that kind of power over you.*

Darius stepped forward, and gathered the now weeping Olivia into his arms. "All right. We'll give this thing a try." He held her close for a few minutes more, then stepped away as her sobbing subsided. "It will be a while before I can call you *mother*, though."

Olivia wiped at her eyes, and gave a teary smile. "Call

me whatever you want. I just want to know you, to have a place in your life."

A glance in his father's direction and he found the old man grinning. "Good attitude, Darius. Ma Beaulah will be proud."

Rashad nodded. "You're a big man, Darius." He walked over and slapped his friend a low-five. "A big man with a huge head."

He punched Rashad in the chest, and he feigned injury. "Shut up, Rashad, before I snatch them 'locks outta your head."

As Olivia and his father excused themselves, Darius waited alone with his friends. In the silence that settled over the room, Darius offered up a quick prayer that both his marriage and his new relationship with his mother would be blessed.

A knock sounded on the door, and Pastor Roberts stepped in. "Gentlemen, it's time for you all to come out." He walked over to Darius and patted him on the shoulder. "You know, I baptized Eve when she was knee-high to a piano bench. Are you ready to marry our little sweetheart and spoil her real good?"

"Yes, sir, I am." He shook hands with the rotund minister.

"Then follow me."

So Darius and his buddies followed Pastor Roberts out of the room.

Filled with the hope of a happy future, he entered the crowded sanctuary. As he, Rashad, Marco and Ken took their places at the altar, he took in the scene. His mother and father sat next to each other on the first pew on the left side of the church. To his surprise, they seemed to be getting along better than they had in years.

I hope Olivia is sincere with both of us. Pop deserves happiness.

Next to his father sat the smiling Ma Beaulah. Wearing her fancy white suit and her best Sunday hat, she dabbed at her eyes with a tissue. Darius caught her eye for a moment, and she gave him a thumbs-up. He chuckled to himself.

The opening notes of "Moonlight Sonata" floated out onto the hushed room. Darius turned toward the vestibule doors to see Eve's bridesmaids begin their processional. Anticipation filled him as he watched them take their dainty steps toward the altar. He stood, in anticipation of his bride, and by the time Eve's little cousins came down the aisle, sprinkling the path with yellow rose petals, he could barely breathe.

The ushers closed the doors. A few long moments passed, and when he thought he could stand it no longer, they reopened.

Framed in the doorway stood Eve, more beautiful than he'd ever seen. The figure-grazing gown fell to the floor in a puddle of rustling fabric. Her sideswept hair, the large flower ornamenting it and the happy sparkle in her cocoa eyes all sent his heart soaring. As she glided toward him on the arm of her uncle, everything else faded away. Nothing existed but the two of them, and he wanted it that way forever.

As Eve was ushered down the aisle by her father's younger brother, her eyes held Darius's. Seeing him there, waiting for her, made her want to run the rest of the way, but she held fast to propriety, taking the slow steps the occasion demanded until she arrived at his side. She reached out with a satin-gloved hand, and Darius captured it with his own. As Uncle Cordell took his seat, the ceremony began.

Pastor Roberts spoke for a few moments on the sanctity of marriage before administering the vows. Looking into Darius's handsome face, she recited the words with all the emotion she felt. His hand cradling hers felt so right, so natural.

When he spoke his vows to her, she could hear his sincerity. The tears of joy slid unbidden down her cheeks as he promised her forever. And when he'd placed the glistening band of gold onto her finger, and she returned the gesture, Pastor Roberts pronounced them man and wife.

He dipped his head, and she received his kiss. Everything she felt for him impressed on her heart in that moment, and she knew that no matter what the future held, the magic of that moment would always remain.

Epilogue

Wearing her thin white silk nightgown, Eve stepped a bare foot onto the wooden patio attached to her honeymoon cabana. Darius and she had spent one night at the Park, relearning all the sweet spots on each others' bodies. Yesterday morning, she'd been snuggled close to him on a flight to beautiful Ocho Rios, Jamaica.

Now, as she walked out onto the quiet strip of private beach that came with the cabana, she enjoyed the feel of the breeze playing through her hair. The sun shimmered on the cerulean surface of the Caribbean Sea mere feet away from where she stood. The water seemed to stretch on forever, and as she inhaled the fresh air, she sighed.

Everything she'd gone through up until now was worthwhile to bring her to this magical place, with the man she loved.

She felt Darius's presence behind her a moment before he slipped his arms around her waist. Pulling her in against his bare chest, he kissed the side of her neck. "Good morning."

Smiling, she turned to face him. "Good morning, yourself."

"They'll be delivering our breakfast in bed soon."

"I know." She glanced out over the rippling surface of the water. "I'm coming in. It's just so beautiful here."

"Not as beautiful as you, baby." His lips crashed down

on hers renewing the passion she'd spent the past two nights unleashing on him.

"Exactly how long do we have before the food comes?" She stroked her hand across his chest, making no effort to hide the desire she felt.

Leading her back toward the thatch roof cabin, he let loose a sexy, rumbling chuckle. "Not nearly long enough."

She followed him into their little hideaway and stretched out on the bed. He joined her a heartbeat later. Weaving his fingers into her hair, he pulled her in for his kiss.

As the haze of desire took over her mind, she could feel the lazy circles he made over her thighs through the fabric of her gown. He pulled away from her lips to transfer his kisses to the sensitive flesh of her bare shoulders and the hollow of her throat, and she sighed.

He moved lower, sliding the thin straps off her shoulders, teasing his tongue over her nipples. She crooned low in her throat as pleasure shot through her like electricity.

He stood briefly, snatching off his red boxer shorts. Before they landed on the polished wooden floor, he lifted her gown, taking her white thong from her. A second later he filled her, and she moaned at the sweet invasion.

His impassioned stroking started a fire between her thighs, and she met him stroke for stroke, her hips rising off the bed. He growled, increasing the pace until her world shattered. His orgasm followed close behind, and he came with a shout, collapsing on top of her.

In the silence, she kissed his sweat-dampened brow. "I love you, Darius."

"I love you, Eve," he husked out.

Their forever was just beginning, and she couldn't wait to see where it would take them.

* * * * *